BIANCA & THE HUNTSMAN

ERICA RIDLEY

COPYRIGHT

ALSO BY ERICA RIDLEY

The *Dukes of War*:

The Viscount's Tempting Minx

The Earl's Defiant Wallflower

The Captain's Bluestocking Mistress

The Major's Faux Fiancée

The Brigadier's Runaway Bride

The Pirate's Tempting Stowaway

The Duke's Accidental Wife

A Match, Unmasked

All I Want

The *Wild Wynchesters*:

The Governess Gambit

The Duke Heist

The Perks of Loving a Wallflower

Nobody's Princess

My Rogue to Ruin

***Heist Club*:**

The Rake Mistake

The Modiste Mishap

***Rogues to Riches*:**

Lord of Chance

Lord of Pleasure

Lord of Night

Lord of Temptation

Lord of Secrets

Lord of Vice

Lord of the Masquerade

The *12 Dukes of Christmas*:

Once Upon a Duke

Kiss of a Duke

Wish Upon a Duke

Never Say Duke

Dukes, Actually

The Duke's Bride

The Duke's Embrace

The Duke's Desire

Dawn With a Duke

One Night With a Duke

Ten Days With a Duke

Forever Your Duke

Making Merry

***Gothic Love Stories*:**

Too Wicked to Kiss

Too Sinful to Deny

Too Tempting to Resist

Too Wanton to Wed

Too Brazen to Bite

Magic & Mayhem:

Kissed by Magic

Must Love Magic

Smitten by Magic

Regency Fairy Tales

Bianca & the Huntsman

Her Princess at Midnight

Missing an Erica Ridley book?

Grab the latest edition of the free, downloadable and printable complete book list by series here:

https://ridley.vip/booklist

BIANCA & THE
HUNTSMAN

CHAPTER 1

"*N*o, you fool!" the Countess of Quinseley snapped at her lady's maid. "The diamond tiara must go atop the crown of braids."

Honestly, how difficult could it be to follow simple directions? Perhaps Lady Quinseley ought to give this girl the sack as well. The chit—what was her name?—had lasted a full fortnight longer than the usual specimens that passed for lady's maids these days, but if even the easiest of tasks evaded her comprehension...

Obviously Lady Quinseley wanted to wear her diamond tiara at its most visible angle. It boasted the finest craftsmanship outside of the Crown Jewels, and fit for a queen. Lady Quinseley knew she looked the part, with her regal profile, ramrod posture, and lustrous hair still the color of spun gold, despite her fifty years. She looked decades younger than her actual age, and was proud of it.

"Goddess," squawked the parrot perched above her looking-glass.

Lady Quinseley smiled. There would be a treat for him later. A piece of apple from the bowl atop her dressing table.

She had always been proud of her looks. Why shouldn't she be? She'd been the most winsome baby from the moment of her birth, and had only grown in beauty every year since. Her late husband, the Earl of Quinseley, had fallen in love with her at first sight, forsaking all others in his quest to make her his bride.

Of course, later the earl had also... but she wouldn't think of that. What mattered was the countess keeping her place as the reigning queen of the ton. Yes, yes, Queen Charlotte was the *actual* Queen of England. But among the social set, no one wielded more power than Lady Quinseley.

All because of her beauty.

"That's enough fiddling!" She batted at her lady's maid's trembling hands in exasperation. "Go and iron the next gown. I'll be ready to change dresses after nuncheon."

Lady Quinseley changed gowns, hairstyles, and jewelry at least once every four hours, and never wore the same look twice. This custom was extravagant on purpose. She was not just the most beautiful woman in England, but also one of the wealthiest. And what good were such riches, if not to make others aware of one's superiority?

The new maid—what *was* her name?—ran from the room. Oh, it didn't matter. The countess would sack her before tea time. There was an endless supply of young girls eager for the opportunity to be Lady Quinseley's personal handmaiden.

None of her peers came close to the countess's beauty. No one did. It was a known fact, and yet, the countess still enjoyed playing her little ritual after every change in clothing.

She lifted her arm.

Mirren, her green-and-red parrot, immediately flew down to perch on her slender wrist. He opened and closed his beak in anticipation of the forthcoming apple slice, but he knew better than to dive into the bowl and attempt to bite one of the fat red fruits on his own.

Nobody took what belonged to the countess without her permission.

"Question?" squawked the parrot.

This was how the ritual began. The parrot had been a wedding gift. Lady Quinseley asked Mirren the same question half a dozen times per day and always received the same answer, as they had done for the two decades of her marriage to the earl. It was one of the highlights of her day, and the reason she loved her parrot more than any human.

"Mirren, Mirren, on my hand," she began. "Who is the fairest in all the land?"

You are, the parrot squawked in reply every single time.

Today, Mirren opened his beak to reply, then tilted his head as some movement caught his eye outside the open window behind Lady Quinseley.

She frowned and repeated her question, her voice harsher to convey her discontent. "Mirren, Mirren, on my hand. Who is the fairest in all the land?"

Mirren flapped his wings, his black eyes still gazing over her shoulder.

"Bianca!" he squawked.

"*What?*" Lady Quinseley roared.

She leaped up from the plush stool before her dressing table and turned toward the window. There, sweeping dirt from the pathway below, was the bane of her existence.

Twenty-year-old Bianca White was the illegitimate spawn of the late earl. Lord Quinseley had declared his intent to marry the most beautiful woman in all the land when he'd first laid eyes on Lady Quinseley... but he had not given up his mistress, a passably attractive Black soprano that Lady Quinseley spent the next two decades pretending did not exist.

The resulting child had inherited the worst of both her biological parents. Black hair like her mother, with the same strip of snow-white at the temple her father had also been born with. Even with the girl's golden brown skin, there was no denying her parentage. Not that the earl had tried.

He'd openly acknowledged his bastard daughter from the moment of her birth, as if the low-born chit were as important as an heir.

Then, when the real Lady Quinseley had failed to give him heirs... No, not a failing. A *stratagem*. Any woman whose best currency was her beauty would be a fool to destroy her figure for some squalling, red-faced goblin. Not when there were sponges for prevention and teas to take care of any unwanted consequences. The earl need not know, and had never guessed. And now that he was dead, the one and only heir... was Lady Quinseley.

Or would be, soon enough. That meddlesome accident Bianca White was almost out of the countess's life for good.

Lady Quinseley turned away from the window and positioned her arm so that Mirren was forced to gaze into his mistress's face, rather than at the abomination below. The bird glanced over her shoulder at the bowl of apples. Good. They were back on track.

"Question?" squawked the parrot.

"Mirren, Mirren, on my hand," Lady Quinseley said, her voice tight. "Who is the fairest in all the land?"

The parrot opened his beak. "Bianca!"

With a shout of rage, the countess grabbed the expensive bird, wrung his neck like a farmhouse chicken, and tossed the colorful corpse from the open window.

She did not flinch at the sound of his body thumping to the ground below.

The countess stalked over to the bell pull and tugged the golden rope hard enough to detach it from the wall.

Her lady's maid answered the summons with shaking hands and a panicked expression. "I'm almost done ironing—"

"Who cares about that?" snapped the countess. "You've a new task now."

The lady's maid blanched, but curtseyed. "Anything you wish, madam."

That was more like it.

"My gown can wait." Lady Quinseley rubbed her pale hands together in anticipation. "Have a footman bring me the Huntsman. I've just found his next prey."

CHAPTER 2

*B*ianca White whistled under her breath as she swept the stray dirt from the stone walkway leading from the fashionable Mayfair street to the even more elegant town house behind her. It was a glorious spring day: bright, blue, sunny, crisp. The sort of day that made the world seem alive, and her soul restored along with it.

That she was wielding a broom rather than a coquettish painted fan was neither here nor there. Being a maid was new. Bianca's lot had only tumbled to this a year ago, after her mother died. She'd lost possession of their rented apartment because they'd never truly owned it, or anything else. Bianca's father, the earl, had paid for everything, since long before she was born. Food, shelter, clothing, education... She had never wanted for anything important.

When a dreadful carriage accident took the lives

of the earl and his mistress, the newspapers filled with gossip... and Bianca's stomach filled with dread. What would become of her now, with no family, no income, no savings, no future?

To her surprise and gratification, Lady Quinseley had swooped in to save her. After the funeral, Bianca had gone home with the countess, and since that day, had never left—save to sweep dirt and leaves from the walkway every morning and afternoon. Bianca didn't mind. The mindless tasks gave her something to do, when she would rather have spent her year of mourning buried beneath the covers of her bed.

Today was her first day out of mourning. Her old day dress with its yellow skirt and blue bodice hung limply on her frame—she had lost much of her prior plumpness over the past year—but it felt good to be back in colors again. She felt as though she were *wearing* Spring, not just standing in it.

That her clothes were no longer fashionable did not signify. Maids were not meant to be fancy. And besides, Bianca had nowhere else to go.

She owed Lady Quinseley a great debt for offering her shelter out of kindness... or, at least, out of a sense of obligation to her late husband. It could not be easy to have the proof of one's husband's infidelity living under one's roof, but Lady Quinseley had never said a cross word to her.

Then again, the countess never spoke to Bianca at all.

That was Bianca's greatest source of unhappiness. As an orphan, the countess was the closest thing to family that Bianca had left. She dreamed of being seen, of being spoken to, of being included.

But as a maid, the opposite was true. She was invisible in every room of the house. Even when the countess threw one of her many dinner parties, the guests paid no more attention to the maids bustling in and out than they did to the carpet beneath their feet or the candlesticks holding the candles.

In moments like that, Bianca could not stifle a tiny little wish to be equal. To be valued as a person, and not a faceless automaton with a broom and a dust-rag.

She wasn't equal, of course. Could never be such. Not only was Lady Quinseley a countess, Bianca was the wrong color and born on the wrong side of the blanket. The earl had done his best to raise her as though she were a highborn young lady, but even someone as powerful as he could not turn her into something she was not.

The door to the townhouse opened, revealing the butler.

His normally kind face was lined with concern. "Miss White, I fear... Lady Quinseley is requesting your presence."

Bianca's blues lifted. "Really?"

Most servants lived in fear of being summoned to the countess's side. It was most often to be dismissed without reference. A pronouncement they claimed the countess seemed to relish.

But Bianca wasn't an ordinary servant. In fact,

she wasn't even paid for her labor. She did her part in exchange for the food and shelter Lady Quinseley had given her when Bianca had nowhere else to call home.

Perhaps this was a sign of good things to come. Perhaps this cold, imposing house was about to *become* a home. If the countess had asked for her, that meant the countess had thought of her. That Bianca was seen, and remembered.

What could be a better omen than that?

She replaced the broom in its closet and hurried up the stairs to Lady Quinseley's private parlor, a shy smile tugging at the corners of her lips.

The countess recoiled on sight of her.

Bianca froze in her tracks, the hopeful expression on her face fracturing like broken glass. She ducked her head to hide her face and nervously tucked the tendril of snow-white hair at her temple away behind her ear.

"You asked for me, madam?"

Lady Quinseley made no reply. Bianca could feel her sharp gaze raking over her from head to toe and back up again, cataloging all the ways in which Bianca was not what the exacting countess had wanted.

All Bianca wanted was to make things warm between them. She hoped for acceptance and dreamed of love, but she would settle for an occasional smile or kind word. They weren't family, but must that mean they could not be friends?

Indeed, Bianca had wondered more than once if

their strained relationship was as much her fault as that of the impeccably dignified matriarch before her. Certainly, Bianca had never given much thought to the *countess* before becoming unexpectedly orphaned and suddenly forced to fall on her mercy.

And even then, in those first days... in those first months... Bianca had been drowning in grief. She had adored both her parents. They had loved her. To lose them so suddenly was a blow from which she was still recovering.

But Lady Quinseley must have been suffering, too. Bianca's mother would have been a stranger to her, but the death of Lord Quinseley must have been a sharp loss indeed. Should Bianca have been more considerate of her impromptu guardian's tender feelings? Was there something more she could have said or done to ease the countess's pain, as well as her own?

"Has that broom given you a hunchback yet?" asked Lady Quinseley.

"No, my lady." Bianca lifted her head and rolled her shoulders back to show that her spine was as straight as ever. "Please don't worry about me."

Lady Quinseley harrumphed. She was not looking at Bianca, but rather sorting through a pile of letters on a silver tray. She held one up by the corner as if its putrid contents stank through the folded paper.

"Mrs. Gladwell," she said in disgust. "An invitation to another of her card parties, no doubt. As if I should lower myself to such vulgar entertainments."

"Mrs. Gladwell?" Bianca repeated. It was such a pretty name.

"Once the daughter of a duke, just like I was," said the countess. "But instead of marrying well, she became a plain Mrs. with enough wrinkles to rival a pug." She snorted. "And to think, she'd once considered herself *my* rival."

"She did?"

"I have no true rivals, because I always win. Mrs. Gladwell learned her lesson, as will… but let's not discuss unpleasant things." Lady Quinseley's blue eyes fixed on Bianca. "How would you like to attend my soirée tomorrow night?"

Bianca gasped in delight. "You mean… Not as a maid, but as an invited guest?"

"That is exactly what I mean," said the countess. "You'll attend to your usual duties during the day, of course, but at seven o'clock you will be free to enter the salon and mingle with my guests."

Bianca's heart leaped. Her chest felt lighter than it had in a year. This was definitely a sign of good things to come. Not only was the countess softening toward her, mingling with other guests meant the opportunity to make friends—the one thing Bianca yearned to have more than anything.

"Thank you," she gushed. "You won't regret this."

"I know." The countess's eyes glittered. "I'm planning to relish every moment."

CHAPTER 3

L ord Harry Lysander, the Earl of Eagleton, sat in one of two embroidered armchairs flanking a round mahogany table. On the table was one half-empty glass of port. On the other side of the table sat Harry's father, the Marquess of Albridge. His glass of port was in his hand, and never remained empty for long.

They were in the billiards room of the Savoy Club. The sole gentlemen's club whose subscription they could still afford.

A precarious position which would soon change for the worse, if Harry's father continued imbibing expensive port like a fire brigade putting out flames. Father and son might have paid their subscription through the end of the Season, but unless something changed soon, they would not be able to settle the rest of their accounts.

Cheers rose around the snooker table as Lord Peregrine gained another point on Lord Devin.

"Have you found an heiress yet?" Harry's father slurred.

"I'm hunting," Harry replied evenly.

This was how every conversation between them had started, ever since the day Harry had idly perused his father's charts of accounts and discovered their money streamed in the wrong direction. He'd made a panicked visit to the marquess's man of business, who had confirmed Harry's worst fears. All Harry was set to inherit were three entailed properties and two generations of debt.

Unless Harry married a proper fortune, and soon.

"Hunt faster," said his father. "Stalk the right prey."

This not-particularly-veiled comment referred to Harry's reputation as a rake. He'd earned the title before he'd understood the state of his family's affairs, and since then had been careful to limit his seductions to widows and courtesans—not anyone he might be forced to marry.

When he went to the altar, it would be to wed the bride with the biggest dowry in all the ton. Although there had been several interested heiresses in prior years, Harry's heart hadn't been in it.

His heart no longer mattered. There were bills to pay.

"What about your sister?" asked the marquess. "You get Christina betrothed yet?"

Harry shook his head. "Tina has politely requested that her 'ne'er-do-well rapscallion brother' stay out of her business."

A simple enough wish to grant. It was easy to do nothing, and right in line with Harry's rakehell reputation. When no one expected great things from you, it was impossible to disappoint them.

While his bashful sister suffered a dearth of suitors, Harry fielded the opposite problem. The entailed estates were a known asset, the nonexistent familial wealth assumed to be in good standing, and Harry's upcoming aristocratic title ripe for the bride's taking.

Every year, a new crop of debutantes threw themselves at his feet, hoping to be the new Lady Eagleton and the future Marchioness of Albridge. Rather than let them down individually, he had let it be known that his heart was cold as the Thames in winter. And that only an heiress would do.

His nickname *The Huntsman* was as much due to his unapologetic fortune-hunting as to his rakish conquests. The gossips couldn't go a day without mentioning one or the other. Rather than scare women off, the unvarnished truth served to attract those who wished to be wed—or seduced.

All Harry had to do was let the cream rise to the top and then take what he needed.

Who cared if the women in his orbit were after his body or his title, and not the man himself? He didn't need to be wanted. Love was for poets and fools. A crass exchange of assets was better for everyone. If he and his future marchioness could not stand each other, they wouldn't have to. As long as she had his title and he had her dowry, they could live separate lives. If that was not the dream he'd once had as a young lad, well, every man had to grow up sometime.

"Pardon me, my lords." An apologetic footman appeared beside the table bearing a small tray. "Message for Lord Eagleton."

"Better be a betrothal contract from a bride," the marquess mumbled.

Harry smiled at the footman—who likely had hoped to be tipped a coin for his efforts—and accepted the missive.

He recognized the handwriting at once.

Harry had performed occasional odd tasks for the Countess of Quinseley. For years, she made a clandestine deposit into Harry's banking account in exchange for him paying special attention to her at some ball or other, in an attempt to make her husband jealous.

There had been no such summons since the death of the earl a year earlier. Harry could not imagine what she wanted from him now, but if she was willing to pay for his time… he could not afford to rebuff the countess or the opportunity.

He rose to his feet. "I'll see you tomorrow, Father."

The marquess lifted his glass, the port sloshing at the sudden motion. "I'll be here."

Yes, Harry thought grimly. That was why *he* had to go and dance to Lady Quinseley's tune.

Luckily, there was no need to hail a hackney carriage. The walk from St. James's to Mayfair was less than a mile, and the weather was gorgeous and brisk.

Lady Quinseley's butler answered the door at once, and ushered Harry to the countess's private parlor.

She sat in a tall wingback chair, regal as a throne, as though presiding over her kingdom.

Harry swept a bow. "Looking beautiful, as always, Lady Quinseley."

She smiled. "I know."

This was no idle compliment. Despite being almost twice his age, the countess was indeed one of the most magnificent women Harry had ever seen. The only person ever rumored to have eclipsed Lady Quinseley's beauty was her husband's long-time mistress, a soprano who had become famous first for her voice, and then for her ability to tempt a man away from a face as fine as the countess's.

Rumor had it, Lady Quinseley had retaliated by arranging a loose axle on her husband's favorite coach-and-four. The next time he'd attempted to squire his mistress about instead of his wife, the carriage had separated from the horses and sailed off a bridge, killing both its passengers on impact.

Suspicious, they said, that the driver managed to leap to safety but did not have the wherewithal to shout a warning to his doomed passengers. Suspicious, they said, for such an accident to occur right after a loud and embarrassing argument.

"They" could say whatever they wished. Perhaps Lady Quinseley was mercenary. So was Harry. He was not here to debate her ethics. He was here for her money.

"How may I be of service?"

She folded her hands over her lap. "Are you aware that my husband fathered a bastard?"

All of the ton was aware. The earl had made no attempt to hide his indiscretion, and indeed had acknowledged his daughter openly, even going so far as to arrange for the girl to make her bow, and to champion her entrance into society.

His untimely death had put a halt to that trajectory.

"I have heard rumors of a daughter," Harry answered slowly.

"She is called Bianca White. I want her destroyed."

Harry blinked. Destroyed, as in... resting in a coffin after a second suspicious carriage accident? No, even if that was what the countess wanted, she was too clever to attempt the same maneuver twice.

That's what Harry was for.

"I'm listening," he said carefully.

"You're the Huntsman. She is your new prey. I order you to bring me her heart in your hands... and break it." Lady Quinseley's smile was terrifying. "I am hosting a soirée tomorrow night. Do it then."

"To be clear... You are not suggesting physical harm?"

"Only to her maidenhead. You are the seductor of innocents, are you not? I want you to ruin her."

"I have a personal policy *not* to seduce innocents," he clarified. "It is the only way to avoid the parson's trap."

"Then you are in luck," said the countess. "The chit is an orphan with no family to force you to the altar. What's more, she is a lowborn commoner. We all know what those are like. You will be of no obligation whatsoever to make an 'honest' woman out of a housemaid."

This was true enough. More than one aristocrat took advantage of his female servants because there were no legal or societal consequences to worry about. But Harry had always turned up his nose at such depraved behavior.

It was one thing to enter into an emotionless contract with someone who consented to the trade —a purse for a title—and something quite different to take the virginity of a young woman who would lose her dreams and her future as well as her maidenhead.

"None of your missish expressions," chided the countess. "I'm asking you to break her heart, not bring the still-pulsing organ to me on a platter for my dinner. Though it does sound tasty"

Harry was not at all comforted by this being the second option to occur to the countess.

Then again, if he did not agree, she would

simply find someone else. "How much money are you offering?"

"Ah." A calculating smile curved Lady Quinseley's lips. "I knew I could count on you."

And she named a number he could never refuse.

CHAPTER 4

t five minutes until seven, Bianca put away her dust rag and dressed in her best gown. The yellow silk was a little loose and two years out of fashion, but it would have to do.

Here in Lady Quinseley's home, there was no one to help Bianca with her hair, so she had been forced to forgo her usual neat braids in favor of a simpler, more natural style. She pinned up her thick black curls and allowed it to erupt in a cascade of ebony ringlets down her neck.

There was nothing to be done about the streak of white at her temple that insisted on springing free as a snowy spiral tendril down the side of her face.

The stark white against the golden brown of her skin made both colors stand out. The combination was anything but *au courant*, but brought comfort to Bianca, as it made her feel closer to both of her parents. They were no longer with her in person, but she carried bits of them in her body. Their memories lifted her spirit.

Bianca had always been aware that the circumstances of her birth would forever mark her as an outsider, but she could not help but hope that tonight at least one kind soul would bless her with a smile. Or perhaps even offer to be friends.

She hurried from the servants' quarters in the attic down two flights of stairs to the ground floor, where her guardian's important guests had already begun to gather. Bianca smoothed her skirts with nervous fingers and took a deep breath. Before her courage could desert her, she stepped into the salon.

The large room brimmed with the beau monde. Lords, ladies, the *crème de la crème* of polite society. They were all wealthier, whiter, more fashionable, more self-assured. The haut ton gossiped and tittered and clinked glasses of champagne in tight groups of two and three and four, never once looking in Bianca's direction.

Cautiously, she edged further into the room. She tried to look friendly and approachable. If she did not acquit herself well tonight, the countess might not afford Bianca a second opportunity.

But gazes slid away from her like loose pebbles scattering down a hill. Bianca's shoulders slumped. She was as invisible in her best gown as she was in her maid's apron. If she did manage to capture an aristocrat's attention, they would likely hand her their dirty plate and ask her to fetch them more champagne.

She caught Lady Quinseley's sharp gaze alight on her for a brief moment before bouncing away like all the others. Bianca's eyes stung. If she had been announced, or introduced, perhaps things would go much easier. But she supposed being invited to join the revelry was more than conde-scension enough from the cuckolded widow of the late earl. Bianca was lucky Lady Quinseley had opened the door to her at all. Just being in this room was an enormous concession.

To give her nervous hands something to do, Bianca crossed to the refreshment table and picked up a small plate with a tea cake. She didn't plan to eat, out of fear she'd litter her bodice with crumbs, but she was not usually offered such delicacies and the warm nutmeg smelled divine.

As she debated breaking off the tiniest corner to nibble, her skin prickled with awareness.

Someone was watching her.

She jerked her head up at once, darting her gaze about the room until she encountered the one face pointed in her direction.

Her mouth went dry.

The gentleman was the handsomest man she had ever beheld. Obnoxiously handsome. Impossibly handsome. A mirage of aristocratic perfection.

Shining black boots. Trim black breeches accen-tuating muscular legs. An elegant black coat exquis-itely tailored to emphasize wide shoulders and strong arms. Thick wavy ginger hair. A blood red waistcoat that sparkled like rubies below a jutting cravat, whose dangerously sharp folds were as snowy white as the rebellious ringlet dangling next to Bianca's eye.

She batted the tendril away, recognizing that she was staring, yet unable to force her gaze away.

The gentleman's sultry eyes did not waver in their singular focus.

Bianca should have squirmed beneath the intensity of his attention, but she was too busy absorbing the sharpness of his cheekbones, the strength of his jawline, the cleft in his chin, the firmness of his lips.

What color were his eyes? From this distance, she couldn't say. Light, bright, possibly blue or green. She wanted to inch close enough to find out, drawn to him as helplessly as a fish on a hook. She could not be so bold. To speak to a gentleman without an introduction would be the height of folly. Lady Quinseley would never allow Bianca to attend a gathering again.

But nor was she capable of backing away. Not even when an arrogant smile curved those firm lips, and the handsome red-haired gentleman began walking in her direction. Slowly. Deliberately. A lion hunting his prey, and she the gazelle pinned helpless by the power of his gaze.

He stalked closer until a mere breath separated the tips of her toes from his. He took the trembling saucer from her shaking hands and placed it back on the refreshment table, never releasing his gaze from hers.

His smooth voice was a low rumble she felt over her skin. "How lovely to see you again."

"I... We've never met."

"Shh." He lifted her fingers to his warm lips, his startling blue eyes never leaving her face. "If that were true, then we shouldn't be speaking to each other. And wouldn't that be a shame?"

"I... " was all she could manage. Her fingers were still too close to his lips to allow conscious thought.

He had kissed the back of her hand, but had not released it, choosing instead to rub the pad of his thumb over the soft skin.

"Who are you?" she whispered.

He smiled. "The Huntsman."

Her heart skittered, then beat twice as fast as before. *The Huntsman.* She knew exactly who this was. The Earl of Eagleton, unapologetic fortune-hunter, and a rakehell of such prowess that debutantes had been known to swoon upon sight of him.

But what was he doing talking to her? She was no debutante, no aristocrat, and certainly no heiress. The opposite of what he should be hunting for. Had he somehow confused her—*her*, with her brown skin and white-streaked hair and worn yellow gown—with a lady of means?

"I'm Bianca," she stammered. "Lady Quinseley's... "

What was she, exactly? The countess's ward? House guest? Servant? Her dead husband's regretful mistake?

"I know exactly who you are, Miss White. Just as

27

I see by the widening of your beautiful brown eyes that you know who and what *I* am, as well."

"Then... Why... " she managed.

"Why not?" His thumb gave the back of her hand another soft caress. "I'm not offering you marriage. I'm offering you—"

"Friendship?" she blurted.

The corner of his mouth twitched. "We can certainly start with that, and see where it leads. Hopefully somewhere pleasurable for both of us."

Pleasurable. He was proposing an affaire.

No one was this outrageous without being so on purpose. His flirtation was too bold, too over-the-top, too *unlikely* for Bianca to possibly take him seriously.

And yet, the undisguised interest in his gaze seemed very real. As if he'd felt her presence as viscerally as she'd felt his.

Nor could she help but be charmed by his honesty. He did not hide who he was behind a mask of manners and propriety. He introduced himself as the Huntsman. He was not proposing marriage.

But he *would* offer her... whatever Bianca was bold enough to take.

"This room is ever so loud," he said softly. So softly, she should not have been able to hear him. And yet, each syllable skated sensuously across her skin, leaving gooseflesh in its wake. "I hear the adjoining room is a library. There are those who claim nothing could be more innocuous and boring than a room full of books. Shall we go and find out?"

Bianca's breath caught. She trembled with temptation.

What if this was her one opportunity? Tomorrow and every day hence would be filled with sixteen hours of brooms and dust pans and chamber pots and dirty linen. What if she would never again find herself with her trembling fingers in the warm grip of a devilishly handsome scoundrel, and this was her sole chance to experience where such scandalous talk might lead?

Only a fool would spend the rest of her life in shadow without being brave enough to face the sun.

She breathed in his scent and curled her fingers about his strong arm. "I believe I might have the briefest of moments to spare. Very well, Huntsman. Please lead the way."

CHAPTER 5

*S*he said *please*.

An icy shiver tickled along the back of Harry's neck. He swallowed hard. A woman this beautiful did not need to say "please" in order to be flirted with, to be courted, to be wooed.

But that wasn't what he could give her. The Huntsman was no hero, no savior, no charming prince. Instead of salvation, all Harry could offer was total ruin.

Yet she wrapped her slender fingers around his arm so trustingly. He was the worst sort of scoundrel, because her trust made him feel strong, made him feel like her protector, when in fact he was the beast she most needed protection against.

He could not take his eyes from her. Her huge brown eyes framed by black curling lashes Her smooth, golden-brown skin and mouth-watering décolletage. Her ebony black curls and those plump, blood-red lips.

Even the twisted ringlet of bone-white hair at her temple should have frightened him away, but instead drew him in even closer.

Miss White's father had been born with the same streak of white. Seeing it on a young woman so gorgeous only made her look all the more elegant and distinguished. She was the daughter of an earl. She didn't need to be born on the right side of the blanket to carry herself with regal grace, and quicken the heartbeat of every red-blooded male in the room.

Most of which were staring at Harry now. Some covertly, others openly. All wondering when and how he'd made the acquaintance of the beauty in their midst.

They all knew her name. With her coloring and the tell-tale shock of white at her temple, there was no need for a formal announcement to divine her parentage. The name *Miss Bianca White* had been known to the ton since before the girl was old enough to say her own name, so proud was her father the earl.

Some thought Lord Quinseley's jubilance would lessen once his countess began to bear heirs, but that happy day never arrived. The earl was content to center all his attention on his daughter. He took joy in her every gesture and utterance, despite her illegitimacy. According to the earl, no babe was sweeter, no child more clever, no girl prettier, no young woman more accomplished than his darling Miss Bianca.

It had sounded like the exaggerations of a proud Papa. Surely Bianca White was an ordinary chit, whose attributes had been embellished to the point of legend by a good-hearted, if misguided, old man.

But now that she was standing before Harry, with her soft hand on his arm, and her wide eyes blinking up at him, and her kissable lips so poutingly perfect... He wondered if the old man hadn't given his daughter credit *enough*. She was prettier than Harry had been prepared for. Kinder, sweeter, more disarmingly charming.

But as for clever... well. She was the fluffy white bunny placing her paw within reach of the wolf.

"This way." Harry used his cajoling voice, his spun-sugar voice, the voice so low one had to lean in close to hear it. The voice that had disintegrated a dozen petticoats and had given rise to more than one meeting a dawn with dueling pistols.

The seductive voice was overkill. It wasn't Miss White's cleverness that endangered her, but Harry's craftiness, his wiliness, combined with her utterly sheltered upbringing. Why wouldn't she place her paw in the trap? She'd never met a wolf before. Never been on a hunt. Never been the hunted.

She didn't know to be wary. A true gentleman would not smile so dazzlingly to distract her from the knowing gazes of the lookers-on as he led her conspicuously from the safety of numbers off into the treacherous privacy of shadows.

As they slipped from the salon, Harry caught Lady Quinseley's eyes. She gave him a subtle smirk of approval, and lifted the wrist from which dangled a pearl-embroidered reticule. Its bulging interior was filled with nothing but banknotes, all of which would soon belong to Harry.

· All he had to do was what the throbbing in his loins urged him to do: Take his pleasure with the most beautiful creature he had ever seen.

Then walk away, leaving her to be discovered and decried, her inconsequential reputation in tatters and his still gloriously intact. Miss White would be shunned from society, tossed from the townhouse. And Harry would waltz back into his club with his pockets fatter, able to pay his father's next bottle of port, and perhaps buy a few more months' amnesty.

An easy trade. A necessary trade. A devil's bargain the Hunter could not refuse.

No matter how terrible the storm his actions brought down on the innocent little lamb at his side.

"Do you visit this library often, Miss White?"

"Every day. I'm allotted twenty minutes every afternoon to clean it." As soon as the words were out of her mouth, her cheeks flushed with mortification at the implications of this confession.

She was not the countess's guest. She was a servant.

Lady Quinseley had not lied when she'd claimed no one would come to champion Miss White's cause once it was made known she was a fallen woman. Miss White was only accepted on the fringes of society as it stood now. She would soon be persona non grata. And, most likely, servant class forevermore. Doomed to wait hand and foot on her betters, despite having the same blue blood running through her own veins.

"But you do read?" he prompted, as if it was of no consequence at all to learn he'd absconded with a housemaid rather than a lady.

"Every chance I get," she admitted shyly. "I spend two of my allotted minutes selecting a new title, which I stay up far too late reading by the light of a tallow candle."

Tallow. The cheapest sort of candle, made of animal fat. Stinky, smoky, godawful. Something only peasants resorted to. Harry was certain Lady Quinseley had never authorized the purchase of a tallow candle in her entire life until she welcomed Miss White under her roof.

Welcome was perhaps a strong word. Most likely, Miss White had been lucky to even be granted access to tallow candles.

The only question was why Lady Quinseley had bothered to open her home to the offspring of her husband's mistress at all. The countess wasn't known for charity and compassion. She was beautiful and ruthless and perhaps the most dangerous of all the sophisticated, soulless creatures in their London jungle.

Take the library, for instance. Lady Quinseley's suggestion. She'd even moved the soirée to the adjoining room so that there would be as little delay as possible between the hunter meeting his prey and setting his trap.

The countess had done most of the work for him. The library overflowed with plush sofas and conveniently soft cushions upon which one could easily destroy an innocent young woman's life.

The worst would be the knowledge that Miss White had come willingly. Harry had told her he was the Huntsman. He'd warned her there would be no subsequent proposal for marriage. His reputation had filled in the rest of the details.

Yet she'd looked at him with such sweetness and longing… as if she saw more than a cold, calculating monster. As if inside the beast, beat a heart of tarnished gold, begging only for the application of a hand accustomed to polishing sullied surfaces. As though she were made for him, and he for her. As though their collision need not lead to ruin, but to a better future for them both.

How disgustingly trusting. How naively trite.

And yet, when he'd placed her fingers to his lips, he'd wanted it to be true so badly, Harry had let himself believe, just for a second, that maybe she was right. That it wasn't the heavy purse in the other room pulling his strings, but the tenderness in his own heart. That this was not a cruel seduction, but a prelude to a lifetime of kisses, each sweeter than the last. That he was not a beast, but his best self. A gentleman who acted like one. A man who did not take what did not belong to him, nor abandon those who trusted him.

The kind of man he might have been, were he not weighted down beneath the ocean of his father's debts.

The kind of man he could still be, if only in this moment, if only to this woman.

Harry had never taken on the role of protector to a non-family-member before. It was hard enough to tread water whilst carrying his father and sister. He kept falling beneath the surface, then bubbling up to cough and sputter another day.

His choices were clear: Destroy an innocent girl, or walk away from a windfall. Disappoint his father. Enrage the countess. Become the next target in her sights. But save Miss White in the process. The clock was ticking.

Both of their fates were in his hands.

CHAPTER 6

*B*ianca's heart raced, as though she'd just stepped on stage to sing a solo without knowing the words to the song.

The stage was familiar. She entered this library every day to dust, to sweep, to slip another book under her arm to while away the long nights when she could not sleep, despite her bone-weary exhaustion.

But the song… She'd never heard this melody before. The promise of a kiss. The flustering headiness of an unexpected flirtation. She hadn't had much reason to sing since the death of her parents, but for the first time in over a year, her life was showing signs of music once again.

She was glad it was with the Earl of Eagleton. With him, one knew where one stood. He was a lord; she was a pauper. His warning that there would be no offer of marriage was superfluous. She hadn't even expected an invitation to attend Lady

Quinseley's soirée. Bianca knew better than to presume herself one of the ton, no matter who her father was.

Even if Bianca had been born a lady, the Earl of Eagleton would still be the ideal man for a first kiss. He was an accomplished rake. He would be *good* at kissing. And there would be no lies between them. For him, it would never be anything more than a stolen kiss. No pesky emotions, no inconvenient feelings, no dwelling on could-have-dones and might-have-beens. After tonight, she wouldn't enter his mind again.

It was just one moment. Here. Now. A kiss she'd never expected to experience. A chance she would likely never have again.

For him, forgettable.

For Bianca… a memory to cherish when her back ached from stooping and sweeping and scrubbing, when her feet swelled from being sent up and down every flight of stairs over and over.

The next time she crawled into her cot in the stifling attic to try to sleep, when her mind raced and refused to rest, at least this time the memory would be one worth keeping.

That was, if he ever got around to the kissing. For an infamous rake who'd unsubtly managed to wrangle her alone in a library, the subsequent moments had been confusingly devoid of licentious innuendo or inappropriate caresses.

If anything, he looked… Not tortured, exactly. Indecisive. Angry. Conflicted. Resigned. Hesitant.

She could not imagine what was going through his handsome, tousled-ginger head. The fact that any thoughts were going through his brain at all was a worrying sign. Was he *not* going to kiss her, after all? Even though he was a rake, even though she'd agreed to his terms, even though they both knew they would have no future together, had the earl suddenly decided there was no point in wasting even a few paltry seconds?

The flattered hope bubbling in her chest flattened and fell. Of course he didn't need to kiss *her*. The parlor on the other side of the closed door was full of more suitable options. Richer, whiter, legitimate ladies without calluses on their hands or fingernails jagged and broken from daily work.

Had he brought her here as some sort of jest? One everyone else was in on? And she, the butt of the joke, the overeducated housemaid who had actually believed, just for a moment, that she might find a place to belong. That this handsome rakehell might look at her as a woman to desire, rather than an object of pity.

That did it. She was counting to ten, then turning away. If she'd read him wrong, if the earl's interest was in embarrassing her rather than embracing her, she would not stand about waiting to be humiliated. For that, she could return to a soirée in which everyone else correctly believed themselves to be her betters.

Or she could take the side door and run back upstairs to her stifling little room and its rickety cot, where a novel full of romance and adventure awaited her.

She took a shaky breath, and began to count.

One…

Two…

Three…

"Miss White." The Earl of Eagleton's blue eyes were intense.

The numbers fizzled and popped in Bianca's head. Was this the moment? Was he about to kiss her after all?

"Yes?" she said breathlessly.

"Miss White," he said again, and took her hands in his.

This was it! She closed her eyes, lifted her chin, and puckered her lips—

"*Miss White.*" He squeezed her hands urgently.

She squinted open one of her eyes, then stopped puckering her lips. His face was no closer than it was before. Perhaps a little further away. And lined with… Guilt?

"Run away," he ground out.

She blinked in confusion. "From you? But you brought me here."

His grip tightened on her fingers. "Flee from here. Escape while you still can. Never return to this house, never return to Lady Quinseley—"

"But she is all that is gracious," Bianca protested loyally. "She may not spoil me with luxury, but she was not obligated to offer me anything at all. If it weren't for her—"

"If it weren't for her, you wouldn't be seconds away from ruin. Lady Quinseley is not your friend, Miss White. She doesn't want you to flourish. She wants your utter destruction, and will pay any price to get it."

"W-what? She... But I... "

His eyes were sympathetic, but honest.

Hurt and humiliation twisted in Bianca's gut. She had wanted *so much* to have a family again. Had longed for her mother, had imagined Lady Quinseley taking on if not a motherly role, or one of friendship, then at least one of companionship.

Bianca had so yearned to be wanted, to be accepted, to be loved, that she'd let herself believe her father's countess would one day thaw toward her, that Lady Quinseley would draw her to bosom in a hug, would say *Your father broke our vows, but I would never blame his betrayal on an innocent child. Of course we're family. I won't leave you.*

"I thought Lady Quinseley and I could be f... " Bianca swallowed hard and started over. "I thought we could be friends."

"Then you are even more foolish than I feared," Eagleton said harshly. "If you stay, kitten, she will destroy you. Perhaps tomorrow. Perhaps tonight. She grows impatient, which makes her dangerous. Lady Quinseley always gets what she wants."

"What does she want?" Bianca whispered.

"Your absolute misery... or worse. Your life could be in danger. There are rumors... But this is no time to gossip. Your time is limited. She saw us

41

enter the library. She won't expect to see you for another hour, maybe two. Which gives you time to—"

"Won't expect to see me! But that means she thinks that we... That you and I are currently engaged in... "

"You should have thought the same when you accepted my invitation. A wiser woman would never have agreed. But I'm glad you did, because it's given me the chance to save you. *Take it.* I'll read a book by the fire while you pack your belongings and hie far away from here as quickly as possible. If you don't leave on your own two feet tonight... You might leave in a box."

She jerked her hands from his. Surely the situation was not as dire as he claimed... but could she be so certain? Even the most forgiving interpretation of Lady Quinseley's personality would be forced to acknowledge her ambition, her vanity, her ruthlessness.

"What rumors?" she demanded.

Eagleton winced. "Miss White... "

"*What rumors?*"

"That your parents' accident was no accident. That their deaths were by design. Vengeance for the crime of adultery. Retribution to right a wrong."

Fear and panic rushed through her.

"I was supposed to be with them that day. Father visited every Sunday after church, like clockwork. The three of us would go out for ices, then take a drive up to... "

Bianca's menses had kept her at home. Bloating, cramps, a pounding megrim. How she had cursed her abominable luck.

"If I'd gone with them as planned, I'd be dead, too."

"She's been biding her time ever since. Keeping her enemy close—"

"I didn't know I *was* her enemy!" Bianca burst out.

But shouldn't she have suspected? Father never missed a visit, but Bianca hadn't even met Lady Quinseley until after the funeral. Bianca had never questioned the countess's absence. What wife visited her husband's mistress and illegitimate child? But it had never occurred to her that twenty years of anger, of resentment, of relentless, flagrant betrayal of their wedding vows would build inside Lady Quinseley until the pressure erupted like lava, destroying everyone in its path.

"Now you know." Eagleton grabbed her shoulders. "We've wasted a quarter hour already. You must run while you still can."

"Run where?" she said desperately. "I don't know anyone else who would take me in. Unless you…?"

"I cannot even afford a kitten, and the beasts feed themselves," Eagleton said dryly. "*Think.* There must be someone. Where can you go that she won't look to find you?"

"Everyone is afraid of her. There's no one who would dare stand up to—" Bianca's voice caught.

There *was* someone who wasn't loyal to Lady

Quinseley. Someone who would love the opportunity to stick a knife in her old rival's back, if only figuratively.

Bianca gasped. "I may have thought of someone."

"Who?"

"Mrs. Gladwell. But she doesn't know me, and I don't know how to find her. It's hopeless. The countess is going to—"

"She won't know. Not if you hurry." Eagleton withdrew a calling card and a pencil from his waistcoat pocket and scratched out an address on the other side. "Give this address to the hackney driver, but keep the card to show to the Gladwells' butler. Fenwick will tell Mrs. Gladwell you've come to call."

"What happens after that?"

Eagleton let go of her shoulders and turned her toward the door. "After that is up to you."

CHAPTER 7

*B*ianca nodded her understanding and fled from the library. She took the side door and raced up the rear servants' stairs to her bedchamber in the attic. Twelve months ago, she'd arrived with everything that could fit inside a large trunk, and it was still standing there in the corner, virtually untouched during the long months since.

The clothing inside didn't fit inside the tiny servants' box she'd been given for her belongings. Besides, Bianca hadn't wanted to ruin the many fine gowns her father had given her by wearing them to scrub floors and wash windows.

The gowns were still there, in pristine condition inside her cedar trunk... and there in the attic they would have to remain. Bianca couldn't lug about a trunk larger than she was all by herself, nor bang the cedar chest down three flights of stairs—even the servant stairs—without causing undue attention.

She was only going to be able to take whatever she could carry with her. A bag! She needed a bag. There was no bag. Blast. She would have to fashion one from... Aha, her oldest and rattiest dress. Quickly, she tied the bodice end into a knot, then began stuffing clothing into the skirt end. A few practical pieces from her servants' box, a few impractical pieces from her father's trunk. There was no way to know what to expect from the future, other than ensuring she was prepared for anything.

A hackney. How was she supposed to pay for a hackney carriage?

Bianca stared about the room blankly. She had no money. She'd never needed any, before. Father had purchased everything she and her mother could ever desire. And then, when Bianca had become Lady Quinseley's housemaid, shopping had been relegated to a distant memory. Her reticule contained nothing but old smelling salts and a faded handkerchief.

There were no coins with which to pay a hackney driver. But Bianca did own items of value.

She flung the lid of her trunk back open and stared in anguish at the fashionable gowns folded so lovingly inside.

For twelve long months, thanks to the knowledge that her old life was *right there*, an arm's length away from her head as she slept, she had been able to breathe. The cedar trunk symbolized all the best memories of her past, and gave her hope for the future. She had guarded its contents as jealously as a fire-breathing dragon protecting its magical cave filled with gold.

But she couldn't take it with her. The past was done. The old Bianca was gone. The new Bianca wasn't the disparate contents of the makeshift bag she was packing, but rather the woman she'd been forced to grow into over the past tumultuous hour.

There was no time for nostalgia. The sand was running out of the hourglass.

With determination, Bianca pulled her fine dresses from the cedar box one by one, yanking off decorative pearls from lacey skirts, and individual stones from bejeweled bodices. In short order, all her favorite dresses were summarily ruined, but her reticule now rattled with beautiful baubles.

Bianca had salvaged enough to be driven right out of London if she wanted... not that anything awaited her out there. Her bits and bobs were worth enough to finance a quick escape, but not the rest of her life. For that, she would need food, shelter, a source of income...

She might end up being a maid for the rest of her life.

Her chest tightened at the realization that what she'd once believed to be a temporary situation might be her future forevermore. A devastating comedown. Father had promised her entrée into Polite Society. He'd promised suitors and outings and holidays to the sea. Acceptance. Comfort. Family. Happiness.

All that was left of those promises rattled in the bottom of her reticule.

Bianca tightened the strings of her reticule and pushed the loops over her wrist. This was no time to wallow. Time was wasting.

She shoved her dancing slippers into her makeshift sack and tied on her leather half-boots. It was too warm for a pelisse, but she shrugged into it anyway. Winter would come soon enough, and she'd be glad for any warmth she could find then.

The novel she'd been reading still lay upon her misshapen pillow. She longed to take it with her. A book was surely a small price to pay for the murder of Bianca's parents. But it did not belong to her, and she didn't wish to be beholden to Lady Quinseley at any level.

The countess had given her room and board, which Bianca had more than repaid with labor. At best, she owed Lady Quinseley nothing. At worst... the countess deserved to spend the rest of her days in prison.

Bianca hefted her sack over her shoulder and hurried down the stairs and out the servants' entrance to the rear garden. Twilight had fallen, leaving the sky a light gray. She walked as quickly as she could without the undue attention breaking into a run would cause, passing behind aristocratic townhouse after aristocratic townhouse until she came to a public street.

In a neighborhood as affluent as this, one might think every household possessed a coach-and-four for each of its residents. Hackneys proliferated nonetheless, in hopes that some of the many wealthy residents would prefer the simplicity of a waiting carriage to the bother of readying one's stabled horses and summoning a private coach from a queue. Even the servants of the wealthy were likely to have the blunt for a carriage ride.

Bianca had no problem flagging down a hackney and climbing inside. Too nervous to give up the Earl of Eagleton's calling card even for a moment, she read the direction aloud to the driver.

He nodded and put the horses in motion.

She sagged against the squab in relief. The driver had asked no questions other than where she was going. Nor had he quoted a price. Her fingers worried at her reticule. They would have to barter an appropriate exchange once she arrived.

Fashionable Mayfair blurred past her window, soon to be replaced by less and less fashionable neighborhoods, until the hackney reached the outer edge of the city, where town houses weren't great brick structures stuck together, but rather individual humble cottages separated by patches of grass or dirt. A large, dense woods stretched out behind the houses. Moonlight bathed the neighborhood in a soft glow.

"Here's where the glassmaker lives," said the driver.

Glassmaker. She hadn't known Mr. Gladwell's profession, but might have been able to guess based on the look of the cottage alone.

While residential buildings in general did tend to have a window in every room to allow in sunlight and fresh air, the glassmaker's cottage was almost a house of glass. Each of the four sides was more window than wall, with a grid of spotless white mullions holding up each sparkling square of clear glass.

"How much for the journey?" she asked the driver.

He named a sum.

Bianca nodded as though the number were what she'd expected, then stared dubiously at her reticule.

How many decorative pearls equaled one pound, nineteen shillings? One? Three? Five? Did she owe him a little extra for failing to pay in coins? How hard was it going to be for the hackney driver to convert these little pearls with bits of string still attached into usable money?

She handed him two of the pearls and scrambled out of the hackney with her belongings.

The driver did not shout after her, but instead shook the reins and set the horses back on their path.

Bianca's relief was immediately replaced by trepidation. Should she have asked the driver to wait? The Earl of Eagleton's card might be enough to convince the butler to announce her name, but it did not ensure entry into the Gladwell home, much less an invitation to take shelter there indefinitely.

But it was too late. The hackney was gone. No others sat idle in the vicinity.

There was nothing to do but continue on.

As she stepped onto the walkway leading to the glassmaker's house, a squirrel ran up a tree, startling a branch-full of bluebirds into flight. A small brown rabbit ventured out from behind a row of bushes, his nose twitching at some unknown scent on the breeze, before he hopped out of sight.

Animals were a good sign, Bianca decided. The woods were close, but not to be feared. There were no predators here. Unlike the den of wolves from which she'd fled, this little clearing was one of safety and peace.

She hoped.

Before she could lose her nerve, she banged the brass knocker beside the door.

A few moments later, an elderly butler appeared. Fenwick, according to Eagleton. To the butler's credit, he did not raise an eyebrow at Bianca's unusual choice in valise.

"May I help you?" he asked politely.

She handed him the calling card at once. "The Earl of Eagleton sent me. Is Mrs. Gladwell at home?"

"Wait here, please." He closed the door, not unkindly.

Bianca switched shoulders with her sack and waited.

In moments, the door swung back open, revealing not the elderly butler Fenwick, but rather a plump, pretty brown-haired woman with laugh lines around her sparkling blue eyes and wide, smiling mouth.

"Miss White, I daresay?" said the woman.

Bianca dipped a curtsey. Of course her coloring and the shock of white protruding from her temple would give her identity away.

The woman beamed as though she'd been waiting for Bianca's visit for years. "I'm Mrs. Gladwell. Come in, come in. What in the world are you doing in that thick pelisse? Fenwick, would you mind… There we go, that's much better, isn't it?"

Bianca nodded. "Thank you, ma'am."

"*Do* tell me you'll stay for tea. I don't know what errand that harridan has sent you on, but I refuse to send you back without a cake or two in your belly. Just look at you! Do you eat anything at all? Heavens, how can I offer you tea when what you really want must be a good supper! Can you spare that long, sweetheart?"

To Bianca's horror, her eyes filled with tears.

"Oh, darling, what is it?" Mrs. Gladwell folded Bianca into her arms as if they had known each other all their lives. "I would say it cannot be as bad as that, but you have had a time of it, haven't you? Losing your parents so young was hardship enough, and to be forced to live with Queen Narcissus on top of it… Has she treated you poorly?"

The whole story spilled out of Bianca at once. Her grief for her parents, her homesickness for a life she would never again have, her new life as a maid-of-all-work, the distance and iciness that characterized her relationship with Lady Queensbury, the unexpected invitation to tonight's soirée, the warning to run for her life, and the speculation as to what evil had been done to Bianca's parents.

"Tell me he must be mistaken," she choked out.

Mrs. Gladwell's eyes were concerned, but not shocked.

"I fear the gossips are most likely correct in their conclusions," said Mrs. Gladwell. "I feared for *you* from the moment I heard you were under her roof. She is known for acts of vengeance, not charity. When she became your benefactress, I could only assume some nefarious plot was afoot."

"I didn't even suspect," Bianca said. "I was so grief-stricken, so starved for welcome, it never crossed my mind that… "

"Oh, why would it? As time went on and you remained healthy, I hoped *I* was wrong, and that it was merely all the old rancor of my youth causing me to unfairly judge a woman who might well have changed for the better at last. I am sorry to have my worst suspicions confirmed."

"Might… might I stay a few nights here with you?" Bianca ventured. "I have no letter of reference, but I am an adept maid in any position. Bedchambers, scullery, laundry—"

"My dear child," Mrs. Gladwell interrupted with visible offense. "I hope you don't think I would put you to *work* after all you've been through. I have maids of my own, whom I pay well for their labor. From this moment forward, you are our guest."

"Thank you," Bianca whispered. The kindness of the gesture was almost too much to handle.

Mrs. Gladwell smiled as if she understood. "My daughters Joy and Gwyneth are only a few years younger than you. They will be delighted to make your acquaintance."

Daughters. Of course someone as sweet-natured as Mrs. Gladwell would have a family of her own. And now a stranger had come into their midst. What if the daughters did not feel the same way about an uninvited guest barging into their cozy household?

Had Bianca finally found shelter, only to soon be turned back out onto the street with nowhere to call home?

CHAPTER 8

*H*arry strode down Bond Street with his head held high, careful to project an image of carefree indolence.

Everyone knew he was The Huntsman, but there was a world of difference between preferring an heiress by choice and being forced to wed one out of necessity. Part of his appeal—besides being heir apparent to a marquessate—was the illusion that a gentleman as rakish as Harry could have his pick of the pack.

Fortune would remain on his side as long as heiresses believed they were *vying* for the opportunity to become his bride. If Harry were reduced to begging for scraps… He shuddered.

All of which had led him to today's mission.

He clutched a small ledger in his gloved hand. It was not the full chart of accounts. That disaster spanned several volumes, each more depressing than the last.

This journal contained the list Harry had compiled of all the open accounts held by the family. The tailors, the mantua maker, the cobbler... The list felt endless, the gravity of its size compounded by the address of the account holders.

The Bond Street Bazaar was the premiere shopping district for the haut ton. The pavements swarmed with aristocrats and the nouveau riche, as many here to see and be seen, as to make additional purchases.

Which meant there was no way to duck into a shop unseen. Enquiring discreetly about the balance of open accounts was going to be next to impossible. But the marquess had left his son no choice.

Harry had attempted to reconcile the accounts via post, only for the responses never to arrive. It had not taken long to realize that Father had directed the staff to confiscate any vendor communications and direct them to him instead.

Which would be fine, if Father applied himself to paying the accounts, rather than deepening the debts. Harry suspected not a single penny had been paid for months, and that its unlikelihood to ever be paid had not slowed down the marquess's spendthrift habits. He had told his father dozens of times to cease spending money they did not have as if they could produce more by wishes alone.

Father had looked Harry in the eye and replied, *I wish you would marry.*

In other words, the situation would only worsen until Harry resolved it. So here he was, pencil in hand, walking shop to shop to jot down outstanding balances. Once he knew just how bad the current situation was, he would know how large of a dowry he needed to catch in his web.

"As large as possible," was all Father would say, which was well and good, but Harry needed concrete numbers. Was there a pool of ten or twenty heiresses to choose from? Or must he funnel his charm toward sharp-tongued Lady Regina, she of the biggest dowry—and cruelest nature—of all the young women in London?

The thought of being leg-shackled to her was enough to give a man chills. That Harry still had a jaunty lilt to his step was because despite the state of his father's accounts and Harry's dismal matrimonial prospects, he hadn't spent any time of late thinking of heiresses like Lady Regina at all.

His head had been filled with images of Miss Bianca White instead.

Foolish, of course. And understandable. No, Miss White could never be Harry's bride, but when he looked at her, he wasn't thinking about wedding bells. He wasn't thinking much of anything beyond how badly he'd wanted to kiss her when she'd tilted up her lips so invitingly. It had taken all his will not to steal one little kiss before sending her away.

He hoped she was all right. She was so pretty, so innocent, so trusting. A lost little lamb in a forest of wolves. Was it any wonder he wanted to eat her up?

Of course, if Miss White were ever to learn of Harry's contract to seduce her for money, she would never have anything to do with him again. It was one thing not to offer marriage, and another to inflict social ruin. Harry was glad to have sent her away. Not just to keep temptation out of his reach, but because if anyone deserved a change in fortune, it was Miss White.

He would do her the favor of keeping his distance. An easy feat, since they were unlikely to cross paths in the future. If her father were still alive, Miss White would receive some quantity of social invitations, but without the earl to sponsor her—and with Lady Quinseley letting it be known that the girl was nothing more than her chambermaid—Miss White's name would be struck from Polite Society altogether.

All for the best, Harry told himself. He and his father were living proof of how dreadful aristocrats were. Miss White would be better off marrying some moneyed shipper or manufactory owner than selling her soul to the beau monde.

If the thought of her doing so curdled Harry's gut with jealousy, well, he'd always been unreasonable. The sort of man who wanted more than he could possibly repay I kind.

The good news was, his encounter with Miss White—and the indecent proposal from Lady Quinseley that had prompted it—had forced Harry to take a long look in the mirror. The soirée might have been the last he'd seen of Miss White *and* the countess, but he would have to face himself in the looking-glass for many years to come.

Miss White's narrow escape from both Lady Quinseley *and* Harry himself had shown him he could not continue down the same path.

It was past time to become a better man.

From now on, Harry was going to be a good man. A gentleman worthy of the title. He would turn his reputation around. No more rakehell seductions was a nice start, but not the whole story. Harry also had to put the family finances to rights. He wasn't yet the marquess, but if Father was only going to worsen the problem, it was up to Harry to fix it.

A task which was proving more daunting by the second. He had visited ten of the shops on his list, and every one of the shopkeepers had managed to produce more unpaid purchases than had been logged in the charts of accounts at home. If he didn't curb his family's spending and soon, Harry wouldn't just need to marry an heiress—he'd have to wed an entire harem of them.

"Good afternoon, Lord Eagleton," said the second modiste on his list. "Why, yes, I provided new gowns for Lady Christina at the start of the season. Such a lovely child, and so nervous about her debut this year. I do hope her suitors are clever enough to see past her shyness."

Tina. Of course she must have gowns befitting a debutante.

The cost was… ye gods. Harry handed the paper back with shaking fingers. He, too, hoped the young bucks were clever enough to scoop up his sister, and fast. At this rate, Tina's first season was destined to be her last. They could not afford a wardrobe this extravagant now, much less a new one next season, and the season after that.

Harry thanked the modiste and hurried back out into the street, where he rested his spine against the tall brick exterior until he could catch his breath. He summed the total debt thus far, and... Good God. Harry didn't just need to marry an heiress. He needed to marry her by Friday.

He knew what his father would say. *Tell Tina she's The Huntress. If both of you marry for money, there won't be anything to worry about.*

But that was a lie. Harry worried about his sister constantly. He wanted Tina to find a love match. The last thing he wished to do was to trap his seventeen-year-old sister in a loveless marriage with some greasy old roué, just because the grasping lecher had deep pockets.

Only one of them would sacrifice romantic love to fulfill his duty to his family, and that person was Harry. He'd put it off for long enough. Time had run out. His hope of finding an heiress he also *liked*, a woman with whom he could enjoy mutual admiration and respect, perhaps one day blossoming into love—would have to stay just that: a dream.

He was The Huntsman. A cold, calculating fortune-hunter without a single heartbeat to waste. The next time an heiress, any heiress, appeared remotely interested in becoming his future marchioness, Harry would march her down the aisle, special wedding license in his pocket. No matter her age, or her intelligence, or her personality. No matter whether they suited, or could even stand each other.

No matter who his heart might want instead.

CHAPTER 9

*B*ianca was perusing the Gladwells' small collection of books in their front parlor when the sound of horse hoofs and carriage wheels crunched to a halt outside the open windows.

Usually, there was nothing more fascinating than peeking at someone else's library. It was like having magic spectacles that could see through their exterior façade to the actual person they were inside. Reading their books was like making friends with their friends.

But this evening, she had not been able to concentrate on the titles before her. Miss Joy Gladwell and Miss Gwyneth Gladwell were to arrive home at any moment. Bianca had carried her bag of belongings into the guest chamber at Mrs. Gladwell's insistence, but Bianca was not at all convinced her real daughters would welcome an interloper into their midst.

Less than two hours had passed, but the wait

had seemed interminable. And now the moment of reckoning was here.

She took a bracing breath and stepped into the corridor just as Fenwick opened the front door.

To Bianca's surprise, not one, not two, but *seven* laughing adolescent women bounced into the cottage like a herd of fawns gamboling in from the woods.

A blond young woman stumbled forward, with a pretty Black woman half-asleep on her shoulder. "Joy, fetch a pillow before Miss Drowsy drools all over my sleeve."

A young woman with brown hair and a wide smile—presumably Miss Joy—motioned them ahead. "Go on, Doc. Put your patient to sleep in the guest chamber."

Doc? The blond girl couldn't be a day over sixteen. None of the young women looked older than seventeen or eighteen.

A slightly younger version of Joy—presumably her sister Gwyneth—fretted, "This is all Miss Peevish's fault. I knew she fetched Miss Drowsy too much ratafia."

"That is *not* what happened," grumped a young woman with dark eyes and light hair.

"Oh, Peavy, you know Goose will believe anything," chided a young woman with golden brown skin the same shade as Bianca's.

"*Achoo!*" sneezed a young woman with pale hair, an even paler face, and splotchy pink cheeks and nose.

"Oh, Rosie." A young woman with bright blue eyes and thin red hair handed her friend a handkerchief. "Here, take mine."

"Oy," The baby-faced blond Doc called out from down the corridor. "There's a lumpy old sack on this bed. Are you certain the guest chamber is free for—"

Oh, blast. Bianca had been so bemused by the seven young women that she'd forgotten to make herself known.

She stepped out into the corridor and cleared her throat.

They all turned to look at her with expressions of surprise and curiosity.

"Er, good evening," she ventured. "I'm Miss Bianca White. Mrs. Gladwell has kindly invited me to spend the night under your hospitality."

Maybe two nights. Maybe twenty. Maybe a few months.

It all depended on what happened next.

"If that's all right with you," she added quickly, lest she not seem appropriately appreciative of their condescension in this matter.

"Well, of course you should *stay*," said Miss Joy, as if the possibility of doing otherwise was too nonsensical to consider. "Help me convince the rest of these wretches to do the same. Doc and Tina have already agreed, and Miss Drowsy won't awaken until morning, but Rosie told Goose her parents cannot weed their flowers without her, and Peavy acts as though her father cannot manage a simple contract without his daughter there to—"

"Pardon me," interrupted Bianca, bewildered. "Am I actually to refer to you all as Doc and Goose and… Miss Drowsy?"

"That's what we call each other," said Goose. "So I guess you ought to as well, if you want to be friends."

"Oh, you're such a goose," said Rosie, and then sneezed. "One of you, introduce us properly."

"Help me with Miss Drowsy first," said Doc.

The other five swarmed around their friend, carried her into the parlor, and deposited her on a chaise longue with a warm blanket as if they'd performed the maneuver hundreds of times.

"Now, introductions," said the elder Miss Glad-well with a smile. "I'm Joy, and my younger sister is Gwyneth, though everyone calls her Goose."

"I don't know why," said Goose with bewilder-ment. "Maybe I have a long neck."

Doc covered her pretty, golden-brown face with her hand.

Joy gestured in her direction. "That's Doc. Her real name is Susan, and she's going to be a surgeon."

"She *is?*" Bianca said, skeptically.

The universities only allowed white men to study medicine. Doc shared Bianca's coloring, and was undeniably female.

"There are challenges," Doc admitted, then lifted her chin. "I will overcome them."

The pink-cheeked blond girl sneezed.

"That's Rosie," Joy explained. "Everything makes her sneeze, including Doc's arrogance."

"*Confidence*," Doc corrected.

"But what causes the worst of Rosie's sneezing fits are her parents' flower gardens," Joy continued with a smile. "Which is why she should spend the night here, instead of at home on the farm."

"She will," Doc said confidently. "She always ends up staying."

"I wish you would let people decide on their own," groused Peavy.

"That's Peavy," said Joy. "We tease her that it's short for 'Peevish', but it's her actual surname. Her first name is—"

"—irrelevant," Peavy grumped.

Joy grinned and gestured to the red-haired girl hanging back behind the others. "That's Christina, better known as Timid Tina."

"Nobody calls her that but us," Peavy muttered.

"My brother calls me Tina," the girl ventured.

"Your brother." Goose fanned herself. "When is *he* coming to stay the night?"

All the others threw cushions at her.

"Mmrrph," mumbled the sleeping girl with dark brown skin and long black braids.

"Miss Drowsy is really Dorothea, and she naps more than any human on the planet," Joy said.

"It wasn't the ratafia. She only had three sips. It's her parents' fault," Doc explained. "Her father is a wealthy merchant who keeps unfashionably early hours. By the time our carriage arrives at a ball, our darling Miss Drowsy is already yawning behind her fan."

"You all go to balls?" Bianca added in wonder.

"Well… We go to certain gatherings," Doc clarified. "Most of us have no noble blood, and none of us have subscriptions to Almack's. Goose and Joy's grandfather is a duke, so they do get invited to most things."

"And they bring us." Rosie rubbed at her nose. "We go everywhere together."

Timid Tina nodded.

"Let me see if I have it straight," said Bianca. "There are seven of you: Joy, Goose, Rosie, Doc, Peavy, Tina, and Miss Drowsy."

"We're debutantes," Goose added helpfully.

"I'm a future surgeon," said Doc.

"Sneaking into the Chelsea Physic Garden to spy on lessons doesn't count as formal training," Peavy grumbled.

"Oh, go edit a boring old contract," Doc replied, undaunted. "It's me you'll come crying to if you take ill."

"You haven't helped Rosie," Peavy muttered.

Rosie sneezed.

"How long have you all been friends?" Bianca asked, laughing.

"Birth," said Goose.

"A little after," Doc clarified. "We all had the same dancing-master, who would bring his charges together to practice figures for the quadrille."

"We spent more time giggling than dancing," Joy

said with a grin. "We became fast friends and have been inseparable ever since."

"Friends share their handsome brothers," Goose said.

"That is not a thing that friends do," Peavy scolded her. "You made that up because you have a tendre for him."

Goose sighed dreamily. "Everyone has a tendre for him."

"Tina's brother is the Earl of Eagleton," Joy explained. "He's called the Huntsman because he—"

Bianca's face was already flushing hot with the memory of her hands in the earl's, and how she'd foolishly puckered her lips for a kiss that never came.

Goose clapped her hands. "See? Bianca has a tendre for him, too."

"If you value your reputation," Tina said quietly, "you'll stay away."

"You should value *your* reputation," Joy instructed her sister, who sighed dramatically.

"Oh, very well." Goose made a shooing gesture toward Bianca. "You can have him."

"Did it not occur to you that Bianca *also* values... " Doc began, then turned her face skyward as if seeking celestial guidance.

For her part, Bianca's feelings toward Eagleton were conflicted. On the one hand, the man known as The Huntsman was undeniably dangerous. On the other hand... he'd saved her. It was because of him that she was free to be here now. For that, she would always be grateful.

Grateful and careful. The others were right. It would be wise to keep her distance.

Perhaps it was best that they had not shared that kiss.

Goose tapped Bianca's shoulder. "Do you want to attend Starry, Starry Night with us?"

"Uh... What does 'Starry, Starry Night' mean? Going outside after dark?"

"Oh, Goose." Joy shook her head fondly at her sister. "Give a little context. It's a ball, hosted by Lord and Lady St. Trevelyon in honor of their daughter Fulvia's debut."

"I... I wasn't invited," Bianca admitted.

"Joy can acquire an additional invitation," Doc said confidently.

"I'm not sure I've an appropriate gown to wear. I wasn't prepared for—"

"Oh, is that *your* satchel on the guest bed?" Goose asked, eyes wide.

"It is. And I'm afraid it doesn't contain anything current." Bianca bit her lip. "I don't have any money, either. Although I did pay the hackney driver with decorative pearls that I pulled off an old gown."

Goose gasped and clapped a hand to her bosom. "There's no defacing *fashion*."

"Miss Drowsy has loads of money," Peavy said. "She probably sleeps on a mattress of it at home, and the excess lumps are what keeps her up at night."

"But we don't need her money," Joy put in, smiling at Bianca. "Not when you have something seven times better."

"What's that?"

Joy beamed at her. "*Friends*. Of course."

Friends.

Of course.

Warmth flooded Bianca's chest. This tight-knit group of friends had accepted her on sight, no questions asked. They didn't look at her and see a rival, or an unworthy peasant, or a pitiful runaway. They saw her as a potential friend.

Bianca's heart buoyed. Their easy acceptance felt like a warm hug. The first hugs she had received since the fateful morning her parents bade her goodbye and set out for a drive in the country.

Hopefully this time, the consequences would not be so tragic.

CHAPTER 10

$\mathcal{H}$arry slumped away from the documents on the wide mahogany desk before him and shoved a hand through his hair. This was his father's study, his father's desk. The marquess should be the one tearing out his hair, desperate for a solution to a problem that had been growing worse for decades.

Instead, Father was off at the Savoy Club, searching for solace at the bottom of a bottle they could not afford.

If Harry had done Lady Quinseley's bidding... But no, that was not an option, should never have seemed a remote possibility. The family might not have money, but Harry at least had honor. He might never see Miss White again, but at least he wouldn't be the cause of her downfall.

Faint giggles sounded down the corridor. Harry couldn't remember the last time he'd felt like laughing. He was glad Tina still could. He was happier yet that his shy sister was actually entertaining friends. She often hung in the background of the group of wallflowers that had welcomed her into their circle, but she had never previously invited any of them home. He was proud to see her making the effort and being rewarded by it.

As to his own predicament... Harry pushed the unpaid accounts aside and lifted a sheet of paper so worn from repeated handling that it felt more like linen than parchment.

The cursed list of heiresses.

His stomach rebelled. He was a romantic fool to still wish to marry... if not for love, then at least some indication of a harmonious future. Was it so unreasonable to want to *like* his bride? To prefer a wife who also liked *him*? Someone he would still be glad to have under his roof after all the accounts were paid. Someone who would be as pleased to beget his children as she was to bear his title.

"Fairy stories," he muttered in disgust.

That future didn't exist for him. Had never existed. Father had seen to that.

If only the marquess had curbed the family's excess spending years ago! There was little to be done about the entailed properties, but the town house they rented in fashionable Mayfair was grotesquely expensive.

But what would the alternative have looked like? He rubbed his face. No Eton or Cambridge for him. No governess and tutors for his timid, bluestocking sister. No gentlemen's clubs for Harry and his father. No tailored evening costumes for them, or *à la mode* French gowns for Tina. No London town house. No fancy chef. No horses, no carriages, no hackney fare. Likely no invitations, either.

Harry and Tina could have raised themselves like stray cats in one of the derelict country estates. Then there would be no chance of Tina making a good match. And no chance of Harry attracting an heiress who could rescue anyone.

He sighed. He could blame his father's profligacy all he liked—and he would not be mistaken—but the truth was, acceptance into the beau monde was highly conditional... and very expensive. If they'd spent a penny less, Harry might not be in a position where saving his family with a strategic alliance would even be possible.

Now it was up to him to pick a name on the list and woo the chit until she consented to be his bride.

The sound of laughter down the hallway grew louder, followed by footsteps in this direction. It didn't sound like seven pairs of feet, which made sense. For Tina's first time inviting a friend home, of course she would only start with one or two. Playing hostess to more would likely feel overwhelming.

The friends must be leaving. From the sound of it, they would be heading past the open study on their way to the front door.

Out of curiosity, he glanced up from his list of heiresses as they passed his study.

Not friends, plural. *Friend*.

Miss Bianca White.

He leapt to his feet instinctively. She stumbled when she saw him, but was carried forward by momentum. In the space of a heartbeat, she'd disappeared from view.

Harry shoved the battered list into his pocket and raced into the corridor.

"Miss White!"

She spun around, dipped a curtsey. "My lord."

He didn't want her to curtsey. He wanted to grab her to him, cradle her soft face in his hands, and crush his lips to hers. It would forever haunt him that he hadn't taken the offered kiss when he'd had the chance.

For Tina's sake, he forced himself to act as though his acquaintance with Miss White was merely casual. Which it was. They'd met exactly once and shared fifteen minutes alone together, in which nothing untoward occurred. Hardly the stuff of scandal.

No reason at all to stay awake nights, dreaming of that library and sweatily rewriting the events to a far more satisfying conclusion.

"You are well?" he asked Miss White politely.

"Very well, thank you," she answered just as politely. But the dilation of her pupils indicated she, too, was remembering that private moment and the path they had not taken.

He shifted his weight. "Where are you off to now?"

Tina sent him a quelling look. His question was

impertinent. Despite his higher rank, Miss White's whereabouts were none of his business.

"The Gladwells," she replied.

Good. The escape had worked. He smiled.

She smiled back.

He felt it warm his soul. "That's much too far to walk. Have you a carriage waiting?"

She shook her head.

This was the moment when any aristocratic bachelor worth his salt—or any gentleman with two shillings to rub together—would offer to take her in his own carriage, or pay for the return hackney himself.

Unfortunately, the carriage and horses had been sold long ago, and the only item in his pocket was a cursed list of the women Harry *ought* to be chasing.

"Don't worry." She held up her reticule. "I can summon my own hackney."

"I'll wait with you until one arrives."

"No one has to wait," said Tina. "There are half a dozen hackney carriages idling by the square at any moment... "

She looked from Miss White to Harry and back again, her eyes widening in understanding.

"I'll just... go back to my book." Tina gave Miss White a sweet smile and sent Harry a look of warning, then backed away to hurry off down the corridor.

At their approach, the butler, Norris, opened the front door.

The sound of rain battering the pavement filled

the air.

Harry swung his concerned gaze to Miss White. "Have you an umbrella?"

She shook her head. "I have not."

"You'll get drenched," he said softly. "We can't have that, can we?"

Her eyes widened.

He had never wanted to kiss her more. Instead, he forced himself to turn to the butler.

"I shall accompany her to the hackney, my lord," said Norris.

"That won't be necessary." Harry took the umbrella from the butler's hand. "I'll see our guest to her hackney safely."

Norris inclined his head. "As you wish, my lord."

Harry pointed the umbrella out into the rain and opened its ribbed canopy. He held it up with his left hand and offered his right elbow to Miss White. "Shall we?"

The moment was reminiscent of their first meeting. Him, proffering his arm, guiding her from a world she believed safe out into a storm of unpredictable nature.

As before, she curled her fingers about his arm trustingly and stepped across the threshold.

They were forced to keep their sides pressed tightly together to ward off the rain. Or perhaps they simply both wished to be as close to the other's warmth as possible. The umbrella protected their heads and shoulders, but Miss White's skirts ruffled in the wind, collecting raindrops by the second.

"This is very kind of you, my lord," said Miss White.

He held her gaze. "I do not have a reputation for kindness. Either the wolf has changed his ways, or you would be wise to presume I possess ulterior motives."

"Which is it?"

"Both. There is nothing I want more than to feel your body against mine. To steal a kiss. To feel your wetness. But alas, your virtue is safe with me. I am no longer the rakehell I once was."

"Since when?" she asked skeptically.

"A few days ago," he admitted.

The look she sent him was saucy. "Pity."

Hunger rose deep within him and he almost kissed her right then and there. To hell with his neighbors, to hell with his new leaf. But while no scandal could fully erase a lord's standing in society, the ton would not be so forgiving to a woman already on the periphery.

"Careful," he growled softly. "I may no longer be a rakehell, but I will never be a saint."

"I doubt you were ever as bad as they say you were."

"I was," he promised. "And worse."

"But only with those who *wanted* your particular brand of wickedness. Likely because of similar predilections of their own. When passion is of mutual consent, where is the problem?"

He stared at her in consternation before recalling just whom he was speaking to. The daughter of an earl, yes. But also the daughter of a courtesan. Miss White's mother had made a comfortable living indulging in wickedness by mutual consent. Lord Quinseley had inarguably been happier in his relationship with his mistress than in the frigid marriage that awaited him at home.

Miss White was the last person who would judge Harry for pleasuring. If anything, she would be disappointed to learn he had chosen to repress that side of himself in order to attract names on a list.

Names he could no longer remember. When in Miss White's presence, he could think of nothing but her.

She gave him a pert look. "My legs are growing quite wet, my lord."

He swallowed. She understood the double entendre very well. "Your legs, or what is between them?"

She arched her brows. "Either find out, or flag a hackney."

It took every ounce of strength he possessed to lift his hand and summon one of the many waiting carriages.

He slanted his gaze down at her. "I quite like you, Miss White."

"In that case, you may call me Bianca, my lord."

"And you may stop with the 'my lord'. You can call me Eagleton, or Harry."

"Not 'the Huntsman'?"

He lowered his voice and leaned closer. "Do you like to be hunted?"

"Maybe I'd like to be caught." She touched his lapel. "By the right beast."

Just then, the hackney stopped in front of them.

Harry bundled her into the carriage, then handed her the umbrella. Rain sluiced down his face. "Don't give that back to my sister. It's my thinly veiled excuse to see you again."

"You don't need an excuse." She blew him a kiss.

The door slammed closed before he could respond, and the driver set off over the muddy cobblestones with his gorgeous—and slightly damp —passenger inside.

Harry stood and watched the carriage recede, oblivious to the cold rivulets of rain sliding down his neck and face.

"That woman needs a protector," he murmured, before realizing he'd made an unconscious double entendre of his own.

A protector could mean a man who paid his mistress for her attentions, keeping her in creature comforts in exchange for satisfying him beneath the sheets. A protector could also mean a true gentleman, someone who kept the unsavories at bay and ensured the safety and continued wellbeing of the protected.

That was the new Harry. The gentleman, not the rogue.

Even if it took every ounce of his willpower.

CHAPTER 11

*A*t last, the moment had come for the St. Trevelyon ball. The theme of Starry, Starry Night had been chosen because the viscountess saw mention in an almanac of a meteor shower predicted for the wee hours of the morning.

According to Bianca's new friends, virtually none of the predictions in almanacs came to pass. This was simply an excuse to throw a party. The point of the fête wasn't the heavens up above, but the debut of Miss Fulvia here on Earth.

All seven of Bianca's friends were also debutantes this season: Joy, Goose, Rosie, Doc, Tina, Peavy, and Miss Drowsy.

Goose was actually a year younger than Joy, but her mother had agreed to let the girls come out at the same time, likely to ensure someone was there to help guide Goose.

"I'm so nervous," Tina said as she pulled the curling tongs out of the fire.

"If you're nervous, put those back," Bianca said in alarm. "I don't want anyone with shaky fingers coming at me with a red-hot iron."

"I'm not nervous about your *hair*. I promise, I'm only giving the white tendril a slightly different curl to make it stand out all the more. I'm nervous about the ball itself. What if no one asks me to dance?"

"Why wouldn't they? You're a lovely person."

"I'm a bluestocking and a wallflower," Tina corrected her dryly. "And no one else in my family is particularly 'lovely'. No self-respecting gentlemen wants anything to do with my brother or my father."

"Luckily, your suitors needn't waltz with your brother or your father," Bianca replied lightly.

But Tina's words made Bianca rethink her last encounter with Lord Eagle—with Harry. He had claimed he was turning over a new leaf. Had Harry undertaken this quest to restore his reputation not solely for his own benefit, but for that of his sister?

Perhaps Bianca ought not to tease him so, in that case. She liked Tina, and would not want to be the cause of any strife for her or any of the others.

Goose tapped her tiny chin as she gazed at Bianca. "We're missing something."

Doc cocked her head. "A necklace."

Joy brightened. "You're absolutely right. I've just the thing!"

She dashed off in search of the perfect jewelry while Peavy and Rosie laced Bianca into the beautiful blue gown Miss Drowsy had loaned her for the occasion. Rosie hummed as she worked, punctuated by the occasional dainty sneeze. Bianca handed her a handkerchief.

The Gladwells did employ a pair of talented lady's maids, but with seven young women to put ready at the same time, the friends had happily pitched in to help each other.

"I'm glad you're coming with us," Tina said fervently. "For us, this is our first season, but you have been out for much longer."

"Out, perhaps," Bianca said, "but not *in*. Even before my year of mourning, I was only invited to the parties where the host or hostess wished to appease my father."

"Half of us are the same way," said Peavy. "My father is a solicitor, and Rosie's parents are successful farmers. We're more well off than many in the ton but, without the corresponding pedigree, they turn up their noses at us."

"The same for Miss Drowsy and me," said Doc. "We're nouveau riche *and* our skin is brown. Two deadly sins in one package."

Rosie nodded. "The four of us only get to be hangers-on because Tina is the daughter of a marquess, and Joy and Goose the granddaughters of a duke."

"Well, there is no one I'd rather be a hanger-on to than all of you," Bianca told them. "Even if this is the last ball I ever attend, it will be worth it because of your company, not the blue blood of the host and hostess."

"Why would it be the last?" Joy asked in confusion. "You're one of us now."

"Your family is lovely for allowing me to stay, but I cannot infringe on your hospitality indefinitely," Bianca explained.

"Sure, you can." Goose ran over to the window and drew back the curtain, revealing a black sky full of conspicuously stationary stars. "Just make a wish upon a star."

"Goose," Peavy said with a sigh. "It doesn't work like—"

"I wish to experience my first kiss tonight," Bianca said obediently.

"Eep!" Goose darted over and clapped her hand over Bianca's mouth. "Never say the wish *aloud*." She lowered her voice. "And that is not what I told you to wish for. Now I'll have to do it myself!"

Joy ran back into the room and fastened a pearl necklace around Bianca's neck. "This sets off your coloring beautifully."

"And matches your patchy hair," added Goose.

"Thank you?" Bianca murmured.

"I'm certain you'll have plenty of opportunity for kisses," Doc said with confidence. "You'll turn every head tonight."

Tina gave Bianca a considering look. "One in particular, I imagine."

∾

BIANCA FELT like a princess when the butler called out her name and presented her to the party. It had been over a year since the last time she'd been surrounded by this many people. Over a year since the last time she wore a gown this fine. Over a year since the last time she'd had the opportunity to dance.

But there was a gauntlet to run first. The St. Trevelyon family stood in a receiving line to greet their arriving guests.

Tina, Joy, and Goose had all independently secured permission to bring friends and had even shared those friends' names with their hostess. But a name scrawled on paper was a far cry from reality.

Bianca dipped her very best curtsey for the viscount and viscountess, then did the same for their daughter, Miss Fulvia St. Trevelyon, and her cousin, Miss Fenella St. Trevelyon, both of whom looked radiant. The women barely inclined their heads in response.

Viscount St. Trevelyon gazed at Bianca with eyes cold enough to shatter ice, but no one stopped her from continuing on and entering the party. Before she knew it, the receiving line was over, and Bianca was standing in an enormous ballroom, buzzing with so many aristocrats it felt like she'd stumbled into a swarming hive.

She followed her friends to the refreshment table, where they selected cakes and biscuits and teased Miss Drowsy to stay away from the punch bowl.

"No napping on the dance floor until after supper is served!"

A quarter hour passed companionably. Miss Fenella St. Trevelyon left the receiving line and disappeared for several minutes, but the river of incoming guests never abated. It was like being at Vauxhall Gardens during a balloon launch.

Despite the distractions of loud music and bustling servants and the fancy crowd, Bianca's eyes were drawn repeatedly to the familiar tousled red hair of a rakish gentleman far away on the opposite side of the room.

The Earl of Eagleton's back was to Bianca, and what a backside it was. Such wide shoulders, such a perfectly trimmed tail coat, such toned legs in their formal breeches and spotless boots.

Harry was deep in conversation with a thin, long-legged beauty with white skin and an aura of barely contained energy.

"Lady Regina Haywood," Tina murmured into Bianca's ear.

"Is she… "

"The Duke of Lennox's sister? Yes. The cruelest person in all the ton? Also yes."

Bianca doubted anyone could be crueler than Lady Quinseley, whom she was relieved to see was not in attendance. The countess tended to stay at home, preferring to host her own soirées, with a smaller, more elite crowd. It was just as well. Bianca had no wish to cross paths with her—or anyone else described by others as cruel.

"Despite what you may have heard," Tina said conspiratorially, "wallflowers need not spend all night standing awkwardly against the wainscoting of actual walls. See those chairs meant for spinsters and companions?" She gestured.

Bianca nodded.

"More comfortable than they look," Joy put in with a smile. "Are you coming?"

Bianca glanced over her shoulder to give one last look at Harry before the handsome earl faded out of her direct line of sight.

His back was still to her, but the young woman he was speaking to stiffened as though she could sense Bianca's interest in her conversation partner from across the entire ballroom.

Bianca couldn't help her interest. She wanted to touch Harry's wide shoulders, kiss his firm mouth. He'd made clear the lines between them, so Bianca knew they would never have anything more than flirtation—no matter what she'd wished upon a star. Nonetheless, she couldn't help but want more. Couldn't stop herself from wanting *him*. Couldn't—

Lady Regina gave her a look of such unconstrained loathing that Bianca gasped aloud at its venom.

"Good God." Peavy whistled beneath her breath. "Did you see the glare Lady Regina just sent Bianca?"

Rosie nodded. "I thought Bianca would be smited on the spot."

"'Smote,'" Doc corrected her.

"Smote," Rosie amended. "Pile of ashes. No trace remaining."

"If Lady Regina approaches you," Tina said to Bianca, "there's only one wise thing to do."

Bianca swallowed. "What's that?"

All seven friends answered in unison. "*Run.*"

CHAPTER 12

*B*ianca's wish to experience her first kiss tonight was looking less likely by the second. The supposedly shooting stars outside stayed stubbornly immobile, just like the popular gentlemen stayed firmly on the opposite side of the ballroom as the "spinster seats" in the far corner.

There was one gentleman in particular who Bianca had hoped would notice her arrival, but thus far he had failed to even turn in her direction.

Perhaps "failed" was the wrong word. Harry hadn't been given a chance. It seemed everyone wanted a piece of the Earl of Eagleton. Not only was Lady Regina practically pinning him in place, but also a constant stream of lords and ladies kept interrupting the two in order to exchange a word with Harry themselves. The poor man hadn't had an opportunity to visit the refreshment table, much less to inspect the occupants of the spinster section.

Bianca, on the other hand, was ready to visit

the refreshment table a second time. Those were some truly delicious cakes. Her friends were already on their second or third round, but Bianca had been taking her time with the first cake, savoring its tart lemon sweetness. And holding out hope that at any moment, Harry would come to interrupt her.

"Anyone want another cake?" she asked her friends.

All but one of them lifted their full plates and shook their heads. Miss Drowsy was already nodding off in her chair, an abandoned cake on the plate in her lap.

Bianca strode to the refreshment stand on her own. She had only been friends with the seven debutantes for about a week, but already felt their absence at her side, much like a general charging into battle without his armor—or fellow soldiers.

"No one is out to get you," she chided herself under her breath.

This wasn't strictly true. Lady Quinseley might very well be plotting against Bianca at this very minute. But the countess was not present at the ball. Bianca could relax. No one might ask her to dance, but nor were they likely to run her through with a sword.

She hesitated with her plate over the array of sweets, then decided on one each of the three most tempting cakes. Supper wouldn't start for two hours. There was to be dancing and a production of Romeo & Juliet first. Cakes seemed like exactly the appropriate fortifying sustenance for a spectator to both activities.

With the trio of cakes balanced in a tower on the center of her small plate, Bianca turned away from the refreshment table—and found herself toe-to-toe with Lady Regina.

"Are you planning to become even *more* disgustingly round than you already are?," Lady Regina inquired. "Perhaps I should warn our hosts that one of their guests is feeding like a pig at a trough."

"Uh," said Bianca. "I took three at a time just to save myself the trip back two more times. If you think my selection inappropriately gluttonous, I could—"

"I'll tell you what's inappropriate. *You*, trying to encroach upon the Earl of Eagleton."

"Am I?" Bianca said. "Then I have been encroaching very poorly, what with me being seated on one side of an enormous ballroom, and him standing without me, far on the opposite side."

"Aha!" Lady Regina crowed. "I knew you were watching his every move. Well, he's not dallying with you now, is he. I sent him off to procure me better wine. One of his friends ordered me a superior champagne from the Savoy Club."

"Isn't this champagne lovely enough?" Bianca glanced over her shoulder at the footmen standing at the ready with trays of champagne. "My glass tasted nice to my palate—"

"What would *you* know? One can tell your class by looking at you—" She made a dismissive gesture toward the golden brown skin of Bianca's bare arms. "—which is to say, you have no class at all."

Bianca's muscles shook, but she ducked her head to hide her hurt, anger, and humiliation. She wished she'd stayed in her chair.

Lady Regina jabbed a finger at Bianca's shoulder. "You shouldn't *be* here."

"Because I'm not peaches and cream like you?"

"*Yes*," Lady Regina snapped. "As if that's not enough, does Polite Society look like the right place for the bastard of a whore?"

Bianca gasped and reached up to tuck her snow-white ringlet behind her ear.

Lady Regina laughed harshly. "There's no hiding your parentage. You might as well have 'Dead Earl's Orphan By-Blow' stamped across your forehead. You are *not* a lady of Quality, and never will be." You're fishing for a protector, just as your mother did."

"Why are you saying all of this?" Bianca stammered.

"You shouldn't need to be told. You should know you're the wrong color and the wrong class. You know you're the bastard of a whore."

"Stop saying—"

"Your mother was a whore, and we *all* know it. A whore and an adulteress."

"She broke no vows! Mama never married."

"Ooh, such an angel. She knowingly took money from a man who did break vows."

"That's—that's what a courtesan *is*. If you think

spending your life looking for and pleasing a string of arrogant, entitled 'protectors' isn't every bit as much work and strife and effort as any other job in Christendom—"

"If you think the beau monde has *jobs*," Lady Regina spat, "then you are as feather-witted as you are out of place. You will *not* have the Earl of Eagleton as a protector. He is mine, and I shall not share him with a mistress."

"If you must physically stop a man from looking around—"

"Oh, he can look all he pleases. Do you believe yourself to be competition? I will be the one wearing his ring and bearing his title. You are so far beneath me that this conversation is as useful as trying to explain to an ant its place in the world before you take your boot and squash it."

Bianca swallowed. "You think me no more than an insect?"

"I think you less than an insect. If I could stomp you out with my boot, I would not hesitate to do so. Run back to your sad cluster of wilted wallflowers if you must. And when you leave, never cross my path again. If I ever have the misfortune of seeing your ugly face—"

"That is quite enough," interjected a quiet, female voice.

Lady Regina whirled around. "Oh God, it's the help."

It was Miss Fenella St. Trevelyon, whom Bianca had met briefly in the receiving line. "Together with my aunt and uncle, I am the hostess of this party."

Lady Regina snorted. "It's not your party. You are the housekeeper. Your aunt and uncle were kind enough to allow you to join them. And I was done with this conversation anyway. I see my rakish, handsome, private 'footman' has managed to procure me something better than this swill you're forcing on the rest of your guests."

She sashayed off without waiting for a response.

Off toward Harry, who had indeed appeared on the opposite side of the ballroom with two flutes of champagne, bearing a confused expression at his missing companion.

With fumbling hands, Bianca set her plate of cakes back onto the refreshment table and let out a long, shaky breath.

"I'm sorry about Lady Regina," Miss St. Trevelyon said softly.

Bianca rubbed her face with trembling fingers. "She hates me."

"She hates everyone."

"She said I don't belong here."

There could be no contradiction to this statement. Lady Regina was right. Bianca *was* the illegitimate offspring of a married lord's mistress. She did have brown skin and black-and-white hair and no sponsor to champion her among the dragons of the ton.

Miss St. Trevelyon gave a commiserating smile. "She tells me that I don't belong, either. Yet here we are. Right in the thick of it. Did I not see you arrive with an entourage of no less than seven cohorts?"

Bianca nodded.

"Then you have found where you belong. With your friends, wherever they are. And frankly, in the arms of any gentleman whom you deign to dance with."

"None of them want to dance with me. Lady Regina said—she thinks—that I am here to find a protector!"

"Never mind what she thinks. Is there a special man whom you wish to ask you to dance?"

Bianca felt her face go hot.

"Then I understand the urge to eat cakes."

"And drink supposedly inferior champagne?" Bianca said wryly. "She sent Eagleton to fetch her better wine from the Savoy Club."

Miss St. Trevelyon looked delighted. "She knows nothing of champagne; the best is already being served, though Lord Peregrine did kindly order more. He admitted his was inferior to ours. The best can be found either here at the refreshment tables, or in the library where my uncle is playing cards with his cronies. Whatever Eagleton brought for Lady Regina, I can promise you came from the worst bottle in the entire house."

Bianca grinned despite herself. "She's drunk half her glass already, and appears to be holding Eagleton's as well."

Where had the earl gone this time? To fetch

"superior" cakes, so that Lady Regina need not imbibe the same flavors as an illegitimate orphan?

She forced her gaze back to Miss St. Trevelyon. "Thank you for saving me."

"What are friends for?" her hostess answered lightly.

The words didn't feel light. They felt like a much-needed hug. And further proof that Lady Regina, while no doubt a quintessential product of her environment, did not speak for all of Polite Society.

"Do you want to come and sit with my friends and me?" Bianca offered. "I am told we are a sad cluster of wilting wallflowers, but if you don't mind absolutely no one noticing or listening to us, there's actually quite a bit of fun to be had."

"Perhaps in a little bit," Miss St. Trevelyon answered, with a wistful look over Bianca's shoulder in the direction of the spinster section. "I'm afraid I am on duty tonight. I *am* the house-keeper, after all, and there has been one calamity after another to sort."

"Has there been?" Bianca said in surprise. "The party seems so smooth."

"Let's hope it stays that way. I've got to go and make certain everything is in place for the Shakespearean production. Meanwhile, I think you might be about to dance after all."

"You do?" Bianca said, startled. "With whom?"

But Miss St. Trevelyon merely tossed her a cheeky grin and disappeared into the crowd.

With a shake of her head, Bianca turned back to retrieve her abandoned cakes—only for a strong male hand to trap her fingers before they could reach her plate.

"I believe this dance belongs to me."

CHAPTER 13

*B*ianca's pulse fluttered at her throat as she gazed up at the Earl of Eagleton.

"Shouldn't you be with Lady Regina?" she asked breathlessly.

"She's had her set."

"She's glaring this way as though she expected another one."

Harry's intense blue eyes did not waver from Bianca's face. "I am standing before the woman with whom I have been dying to dance all evening. If your dance card is full… "

She saw no point in playing coy. "You must know that it is not."

"All that proves is that we are surrounded by fools." He wrapped her hand about his arm and turned toward the dance floor. "Come, make me the most envied of men."

"But Lady Regina—"

"Must we talk about other women?"

"She thinks you're going to offer for her."

He did not deny it. "At this precise moment, what I can offer is a dance, and the person I would most like to dance with is you. You do have the right to say no, of course."

Bianca had no wish to refuse a dance with the man she'd been thinking about without cease, ever since their first encounter. Even knowing Lady Regina was right, that Bianca wasn't good enough to be one of them, that when Harry wed, it would be Lady Regina he met at the altar... None of that quenched her desire to know, at least once, what it felt like to dance in his arms.

She inclined her head. "I believe I can spare twenty minutes of my busy evening."

"I am delighted to hear it. I believe this is to be the last dance before the play, and then supper."

The music changed. A waltz! Could Bianca really be so lucky?

Yet she paused. According to Goose, young ladies of the ton were not allowed to waltz until the patronesses of Almack's bestowed their official permission.

Bianca was so far beneath the patronesses' notice as to be a spot of dust on their hems, and there was no possibility whatsoever of her acquiring a subscription to the assembly rooms or direct approbation.

Which meant, no, she didn't have "permission". And she also didn't give a fig about it. Besides, what could the patronesses do if they learned of this minor rebellion? Bar her from entering a building she was already prohibited from visiting? As Lady Regina had so blatantly pointed out, Bianca was *not* a young lady of the ton. Neither their strictures nor their social punishments applied to her.

She was free to waltz with the Earl of Eagleton if she wished.

And, *oh*, did she wish! She took his arm with enthusiasm.

As he led her onto the floor, Bianca wished on every star up in the sky that Harry would be the one to give her her first kiss. Perhaps such a wish was impertinent, if he indeed intended to betroth himself to Lady Regina. Perhaps Bianca was no better than her mother, who had been head over heels in love with her highborn protector since long before the earl had wed Lady Quinseley.

But Harry wasn't married yet. No vows had been spoken, other than the warning that he could make her no promises. Until he signed betrothal papers, he belonged to no one. Which meant, for the next twenty minutes…

He was hers.

Bianca tried to memorize every new sensation as it occurred. The Earl of Eagleton catching her hand in his. Harry placing his other hand around her back protectively. Her fingertips touching his shoulder. The swing of their hips and the whirl of the room as he led her into the waltz.

"You look ravishingly beautiful," he murmured into her ear.

"Mmm, prove it," she whispered back.

His eyes darkened with desire.

A frisson of power tickled over her skin, making her feel bold and feminine and seductive. The Huntsman was the most notorious rake of the ton. He could entice anyone he pleased. And it was her in his arms, smiling up at him with her eyes from beneath her lashes.

He pulled her a little closer.

"Tut-tut," she teased. "One must think about propriety."

"I cannot think about anything when I am this close to you."

She trailed her finger across his lapel. "Nothing at all?"

"All right, yes. Several possibilities spring to mind, none of which would be condoned on a dance floor. For now, I must rein in my desires and console myself with holding you a few inches closer than is considered proper."

"'For now,'" she repeated. "Does that mean we're to have a 'later'?"

"I bloody hope so," he muttered.

She grinned at him. "I have it on very good authority that the best way to achieve one's desires is to wish it upon a falling star."

"Have you seen any of the alleged falling stars?"

"I have not," Bianca admitted. "Therefore, I have taken the alternative step of wishing upon each and every stationary star in the sky."

"Oh?" Harry smiled wolfishly. "And what was your wish?"

"Ah-ah-ah." She wagged a finger. "I'm assured it won't come true if I tell."

"Forgive me if I doubt the veracity of your advisor. Past experience has shown me that the easiest way for me to grant a woman's wishes is for her to tell them to me directly."

She arched her brows. "How presumptuous to presume my wishes are about *you*."

"They had better be," he growled and hauled her a little closer. "All of mine are about you."

"*All* of them?" she asked pointedly.

He winced. "All that I would choose for myself of my own volition. There are paths I must take for duty, but believe me, I would not wish those circumstances on anyone."

"Might I ask... " She hesitated, then plunged ahead. "Just what are your circumstances?"

He guided them in long, loping circles for a long moment in silence, then let out his breath. "I am not a huntsman out of avarice. I am a fortune-hunter out of necessity. The ton does not fathom the depths of my family's debts. They've no idea."

"You've only told me?"

"It doesn't feel like there's anything 'only' about you. I find I hold your esteem just as highly as that of my peers."

"Oh, I don't *esteem* you," she teased. "I just want you to do unspeakable things with me."

"I can speak them," he promised. "I can kiss things, and lick them, and stroke them—"

"Then what are we waiting for?" She lowered her voice. "Toss the champagne and the biscuits asunder and have your wicked way with me atop the refreshment table."

"Believe me, if I could have my cake and eat it, too…"

His blue gaze was so intense, Bianca could almost feel the ribbons of her gown untying themselves in anticipation.

"Unfortunately, you may recall I've turned over a new leaf," he said as though it pained him. "Even a future marquess must keep to certain standards of behavior if he wishes to wed a certain sort of lady."

"A lady like… Regina?"

Harry did not answer.

Jealousy twisted inside of Bianca. "What a pity it would be if you failed to land such a paragon of Quality and graciousness."

"It would be a disaster," he muttered. "More's the pity."

"A disaster if you marry her, or a disaster if you do not?"

"Probably both," he admitted. "But one outcome saves my sanity, and the other saves my family. There is no choice to be made in the matter."

No, she supposed not. Men like him—lords like her father—always chose their title over their heart. Father had been every bit in as much love with Mother as Mother was with Father, and yet he had never considered the possibility of making his courtesan a bride.

It wasn't even because the earl had been hunting an heiress. He'd been very popular and rich as Croesus. If anyone could have married for love and got away with it, it would have been the Earl of Quinseley.

But, no. There was the title to consider. His duty to wed an *appropriate* wife.

He'd chosen Lady Quinseley for the role. The prettiest lady in the beau monde... if not the most beautiful woman in London. That honor went to Bianca's mother alone.

But beauty wasn't enough. Love wasn't enough.

And so all four of them had been miserable for twenty long years: Father, Mother, Lady Quinseley, and Bianca. In the name of duty. In the name of propriety. In the name of fulfilling society's expectations.

Bianca was suddenly viscerally *glad* not to have been born into a class that doomed her to misery. If the footman refilling the champagne asked her to be his bride, she could say yes. If the Prince Regent himself were to call her into his palace to beg for her hand, she would also be able to say yes.

But when it came to the Earl of Eagleton... Bianca was not the one bound by society's restrictions. For all Harry's privilege, of the two of them only *she* was free to follow her heart.

Even if it led into heartbreak.

CHAPTER 14

*H*arry felt dizzy—and not because of the waltz. Indeed, he could not have asked for a better dance partner. Bianca's steps were graceful, her touch light, her every movement in perfect synchronicity with his own.

It was the subject matter of their conversation that had him at sixes and sevens.

When was the last time he'd been so open and honest with another person? That was an easy question to answer: Never.

Years of fleeting rakish dalliances lent themselves to the baring of naked bodies, not a heart-to-heart baring of souls. As for the peers he'd known since Eton, well, those were the last lads with whom he could share his anxiousness about the state of his father's finances and his fears for the family's future.

He couldn't even *say* the words "anxious" or "afraid". An accomplished rakehell did not suffer such common emotions as "anxiousness" and "fear". A gentleman did not burden others. A lord was too secure in his rightful place at the top of the kingdom to bother looking down his nose at matters so insignificant as the state of his purse.

An earl did not *fret*.

But he'd confessed the truth to Bianca. Not because the circumstances of her birth placed her outside the "legitimate" circles of aristocracy, but because of the kind of person she was, and how safe she made him feel.

Ironic that an heir to a marquessate, who need never worry about having a roof over his head because he possessed not one, not two, but *three* entailed estates that could not be taken from him... should find solace in the comforting gaze of a homeless orphan who paid for hackney carriages with bits torn off her own gown.

And yet, her compassionate brown eyes and her unabated teasing made him feel like she saw him, and understood him, and that none of the things he'd spent a lifetime trying to hide mattered to her in the least. She listened when the topic was serious, and flirted when it was not, accepting both parts of him as a single whole.

In a strange way, they were now on equal footing. He had met her knowing the "worst" of her past, yet was seeing her at her best: resplendent in a yellow-and-blue evening gown, the most gorgeous woman by far at the viscountess's fête.

Bianca could not hide her past from him if she'd

wished to. It was there, in the shock of white at her temple, in the color of her skin, in the gossip columns of cheap newspapers.

And now Henry had shown hi true self to her. Not the carefully crafted rakish lord image talked about by the ton, but the concerned brother, the panicked heir, the future groom dreading endless decades of a loveless marriage.

He was more than he appeared to be at first glance. Just like Bianca.

Tonight, she looked like a princess. A long, flowing gown of robin's-egg-blue that stood out among the relentless pastels of the debutantes. A string of fat white pearls at her throat that enhanced the creamy golden brown of her skin. Her long black hair twisted up high on her head in a pile of braids that exploded into a waterfall of curls. The snow-white ringlet framing half her face bounced becomingly as they whirled through the beats of the waltz. Her blood-red lips, so plump and kissable, were eclipsed only by the flash of straight white teeth when he was fortunate enough to receive one of her stunning smiles.

He could imagine a man spending the rest of his life working to earn those magical smiles. Reveling in victory at each flicker of amusement, then capturing that lush mouth with his own.

How Harry wished they were not waltzing in a crowded ballroom, but rather on an empty balcony that led to a bedchamber! That when their twenty minutes were up, he need not hand her off to someone else, but instead entwine his fingers with hers and tumble onto the nearest mattress. That the only music would come not from an orchestra, but the sounds of two lovers gasping and panting and sighing in pleasure.

A smile quirked the corners of her lips.

His focus sharpened. "What is it?"

Her smile grew wider. "You're looking at me as if you were thinking about ravishing me."

"I'm always thinking about ravishing you. No matter what expression I'm making, rest assured that the only things in my head are extremely detailed plans about what I'd do if we were alone with nothing in our way but a few layers of clothing."

"I don't know what I want more," she murmured. "For you to tell me those very detailed plans, or to be surprised when I find out in person."

God, had there ever been a woman more tempting? Eve had plucked an apple for Adam, but Bianca *was* the forbidden fruit. Harry wanted to lick her, nibble her, eat her, until their lovemaking consumed them both.

He could practically feel Lady Regina's gaze boring into him. Reading his desire for Bianca and swirling into a rage.

Harry did his best to school his expression and control his emotions. It was better for both of them that way. He desired Bianca, he *liked* her, he respected her, but he could not let lust or even a blossoming friendship prevent him from achieving the only goal that mattered: securing his family's future.

He could not allow himself to stray from that path. His father was counting on him. His sister was counting on him. His future children were counting on him.

No matter how much he wanted to twirl Bianca out of the ballroom and into the night sky in order to find a nice patch of soft grass upon which to make his most debauched dreams a reality...

Those were just dreams, and could never be anything more.

"Are you staying safe?" he asked her, urgently. He could not be her protector in the sense he most desired, but he would be her champion in every way that he could.

She gave him a quizzical look. "I'm safe. Mrs. Gladwell won't accept a penny for her hospitality. I've seen no sign of Lady Quinseley."

"You will," he warned her. "She might not have known where to look for you before, but here you are, waltzing with a lord in a ball hosted by her peers. She will have the news by breakfast, and she will not be pleased to receive it."

Bianca looked alarmed. "Of course you're right. I had not thought of her. My life was topsy-turvy with new friends who filled my head with shooting stars and happy-ever-afters. I suppose this must be my last such outing."

Would that be enough to avoid retribution? Once the Countess of Quinseley learned the location of her erstwhile ward, there would be little to stop her from enacting vengeance on Bianca for having the audacity to flee before she was ruined.

Harry hoped Lady Quinseley would console herself with Bianca living on the margins, knowing she would spend every day thereafter stifling her desire to be part of this world, choosing instead to cower in seclusion out of fear of the countess's power.

If that sacrifice *wasn't* enough…

Harry longed to pull Bianca tight against his chest, to wrap his arms about her, to protect her with his name, his title, and his body. He wanted more than to feel her soft curves pressed against him. He wanted her to use him however she liked. As a shield, as a toy, as a lover. He wanted to deflect all of society's arrows with his own skin if that was what it took to keep her safe. To keep her close. To make her his.

But the music ended, and he was forced to let her go. It was time for the play, then supper. Assigned seating and banal small talk with perfectly fine women who were not the one Harry wanted.

"Come." He placed her hand on his arm. "I'll return you to your friends."

"Don't do it," she said quietly.

He looked at her, startled. "No?"

"Don't marry her. Not if you don't wish to. There has got to be a better choice than spending the rest of your life in misery."

"That's a fairy tale. Sometimes there is no other choice."

"For me, perhaps. You're a man. A gentleman, with white skin and noble birth. You have more than a title. You've the world at your feet. If even *you* cannot take it… "

"My duty must always be to—"

"You're more than that, Harry. You're a human being worthy of love."

How he wished that were true. How he wished such a future were possible. How he wished a shooting star really would streak across the night sky, and that granting wishes were as easy as silly fantasies claimed.

But as he gazed into Bianca's eyes, a new question formed. If there *was* such a thing as magic, if Harry were given exactly one wish which was guaranteed to come true…

Would he spend it on himself, or take the opportunity to provide for Bianca? Protecting her once and for all?

CHAPTER 15

*A*fter supper, Bianca reunited with her friends in the far corner of the ballroom with the comfortable chairs. The refreshment table had been restocked, but after eating so many delicious courses, there was no room left in her stomach for so much as a crumb of cake.

The orchestra took their positions and began to play. At first it was hard to hear them over the buzz of gossip about the hosts' daughter Miss Fulvia standing in for a professional actress in the production of Romeo and Juliet and equally unexpected engagement to the dashing Lord Peregrine.

But as soon as it became clear that the orchestra was playing one of the most popular quadrilles of the moment, the guests flocked to the dance floor in droves to make the high-spirited figures.

"*Bianca,*" Goose stage-whispered loudly, giving Bianca's wrist several urgent tugs.

"Goose," said Peavy, "that is the least subtle nudge I have ever seen in my life."

"But she's not looking, and he's coming this way!"

"Who's coming this way?" Bianca's heart beat faster. "Is it Eagleton?"

She started to turn and look.

"Don't turn, don't turn!" Goose latched onto Bianca's arm like a barnacle. "He'll know you're looking for him."

"I *am* looking for him."

"You'll find him in approximately ninety seconds," Doc said wryly. "At his current course, a collision is imminent."

Joy beamed happily. "The Huntsman has had eyes for no one but Bianca all night."

Rosie sneezed and rubbed her nose. "Won't dancing twice in one night turn heads?"

"No," Peavy said flatly. "Everyone knows he'll never marry her."

Bianca's giddy anticipation dimmed.

"No offense meant," Doc put in, indicating her agreement with Peavy's assessment.

"No offense taken," Bianca said with a sigh. "One cannot argue with facts."

"It's not *you*," Joy interjected with an encouraging smile.

"I mean… It *is* you," Peavy said. "He's looking for a very specific type of woman, and you are not it."

Miss Drowsy yawned. "Are we certain Eagleton

is thinking about marriage? One presumes an infamous rakehell only has one thing on his mind."

Goose leaned toward Bianca. "She's alluding to the act of—"

"I followed," Bianca assured her. To be fair, the scandalous idea of making love to Harry was never far from Bianca's thoughts as well. "Don't worry. I know who and what he is."

"So do we. That's why I worry." Tina's voice was quiet, and her eyes serious. "I don't want you to get hurt."

"He'd never hurt me," Bianca said.

Peavy did not look convinced. "A man needn't *intend* to hurt you, in order to hurt you."

"Say what you will," said Bianca, "I trust him. He has been nothing but honest with me from the moment we met. I fully understand that what rules him is not his heart, but his—"

Goose trod heavily upon her toe.

Bianca snapped her teeth closed.

Harry stepped into view, his blue eyes trained on Bianca as if the rest of the ballroom did not exist. "Are you spoken for this set?"

Bianca's dance card was as empty now as it had been when she first arrived.

"I suppose I could spare another moment of my busy schedule," she answered.

His eyes glittered as though she had just promised to present herself nude in a tub dotted with rose petals.

"Shall we go somewhere more private?" He

offered her his arm. "Perhaps a turn about the garden?"

"Oh, well done," Joy murmured. "A second set away from the prying eyes of gossips."

Bianca hoped Goose trod upon her sister's toes as well.

She wrapped her hand around the hard muscle of Harry's upper arm and allowed him to escort her out of the ballroom through the open sash-windowed doors to the rear garden outside.

The night sky was inky black and spattered with stars. With the afternoon spring drizzle that had fallen earlier, Bianca had feared the sky would be too overcast tonight to see much of anything beyond the moon, and was gratified to be proven wrong.

The soft breeze carried a light chill, so she held on tighter to Harry's arm, pressing herself against the warmth of his side.

"Come with me," he murmured into her ear. "I know where we can go."

"A secret trysting corner of the St. Trevelyon garden?" she asked archly, torn between envy of all the other women he might have brought there, and delight that they need not spend the rest of their second and final precious twenty-minute set being stared at by gossips.

"You'll see," was all he would say.

She matched her steps to his, hurrying to keep pace. They followed a stone path around a curve, then abandoned the walkway completely, choosing instead to duck between trees and behind a hedgerow until they emerged in a wide, empty strip on the other side.

"What is this?" she asked.

"The road to the mews. It'll be empty for hours. All the guests have already arrived, and none will call for their carriages until after the dancing ends."

"You mean… We could stand out here past our twenty-minute limit, if we wished to?"

His eyes held hers. "I'm yours for as long as you want me."

Good heavens. That answer certainly sounded like a wish come true. She darted a glance at the stars. Still motionless.

Bianca sighed. Her twenty-first birthday was in a week. For the child of a courtesan, never-been-kissed Bianca was not living up to the family repu-tation. She knew better than to yearn for a different life, but was one magical moment too much to ask?

"What's wrong?" Harry asked with concern.

"I have been waiting all evening to wish upon a shooting star, and fear my wait has been in vain."

"Never trust an almanac," he agreed. "Tomorrow is probably supposed to rain frogs."

"I should like to miss that," she said wryly.

"I am sorry you must miss the shooting star as well. What were you going to wish for?"

"Since I shan't have the opportunity to do it properly, I suppose I might as well tell you." She tilted her head. "I wanted you to kiss me."

"Did you?" he said with interest.

"But I've changed my mind."

His eager expression fell. "And why is that?"

"Because I've decided to grant my own wishes instead of waiting on the heavens. Or on the vexingly slow wits of supposedly insatiable rakes."

His lips twitched. "By which, you mean... ?"

"I'm going to kiss *you*."

He widened his twinkling eyes. "How very rakish!"

She nodded gravely.

He touched his free hand to his cravat as if shocked. "I'm quite scandalized."

"Be scandalized and silent," she scolded him. "Your mouth is easier to kiss when it's not talking."

He closed his lips, then opened them again. "Are we about to engage in a closed-mouth kiss, or an open-mouthed kiss?"

She frowned and tilted her head. "What's an open-mouthed kiss?"

"Ah." He smiled. "Permission to kiss you back, however I like, after you finish kissing me in your manner?"

"Granted," she replied primly.

"All right, then." He lowered his head toward hers. "I'm ready."

"Good," she whispered, then pressed her lips to his.

His lips were firm, yet gentle. Warm, and welcoming. It was quite literally a wish come true. And yet... she could not help but suspect that something important was missing. That he was toying with her. That the Huntsman was biding his time until he could unleash his true passion on his prey.

"Very well," she murmured against his lips. "Show me your way."

His gaze sharpened. "As you wish."

He cupped his hands about her upturned face and slanted his parted lips over hers, nudging and coaxing until her mouth opened to his. He swept his tongue inside to battle with hers, tasting, claiming, teasing.

She could feel each stroke of his tongue as if it passed over every hidden curve and valley of her body. The chills tickling along her skin had nothing to do with the brisk spring weather and everything to do with the heat emanating from the handsome rake before her.

This was not a kiss, but a lesson. A claiming. His very essence branded upon her soul, as hers did the same to his. Two wild things, untamed and free.

"Bianca." His voice was a soft growl, a mingling of breath. "Open your eyes."

Her eyes sprang open... and dazzled to see the heavens afire with streaks of white. The meteor shower! It had come true, just as the almanac had foretold.

She laughed in delight as Harry twirled her down the empty road, waltzing without music to the tune of wishes coming true all over England.

Even though she knew it was foolish, even though she knew magic did not really exist, nothing in this moment was more real than the wishes all around them and the music of their laughter as they danced in each other's arms beneath the shooting stars.

"What do you think?" he asked. "Was it worth the wait?"

In answer, she wrapped her arms about his neck and kissed him with all the passion in her heart.

CHAPTER 16

arry knew he was in trouble the moment his lips touched Bianca's.

He had wanted to kiss her for so long. Before he'd even met her; from the moment he'd glimpsed her across a crowded parlor. Holding back and warning her away had only heightened his desire to taste her lips. He'd thought about it so often and built it into such a tower of yearning that there was no hope of reality living up to his fantasy.

Except it did, and more. She was everything he had longed for. Her kiss was sweeter than expected, her curves softer, her skin warmer, her taste so perfect that he never wanted to come up for breath. The meteor shower lighting the sky with magic was nothing compared to the fireworks going off in his heart.

This was no mere kiss. This was proof that Harry would never be able to walk away. Not without looking over his shoulder every other step, and then giving up and running back to scoop her into his arms to lose himself in another incredible kiss.

The problem was that she was not some idle rakish conquest, a woman whose name he did not know, and it did not matter whether her personality meshed with his.

He *did* know Bianca. He liked her as a person, not as a passing fancy. Lady Quinseley could not have been more wrong when she'd selected Harry to seduce and abandon Bianca. He was the one seduced. The one most likely to be left behind.

After all, he could not offer her any of the things a woman in her position was looking for. Not the financial arrangement of mistress and protector, and certainly not marriage. Oh God, why was he thinking of *marriage*?

He knew what was expected of him. Knew there was only one path out of the darkness for his family, and that Harry was the only one who could walk it. He knew the names of every dowries debutante by heart, ranked in descending order of fortune. Knew the future of the marquessate lay in an alliance with Lady Regina, not a penniless orphan whose pockets were as empty as his own.

And yet, with every kiss, his heart imagined a hundred more. Early morning kisses, so half-asleep they felt like a continuation of his dreams. Kisses before every meal, and after. Kisses while bathing, while reading, while in a hackney. Kisses before bed. Kisses in the middle of the night.

None of those kisses were destined for him, no matter how ardently he might long for them. He knew what lie in wait for him in his own future. If he truly cared for Bianca, there was only one thing he could honorably wish for.

Without breaking their kiss, he closed his eyes as tight as he could and wished upon every one of the shooting stars for the heavens to grant *Bianca's* wishes.

He wished for her to find security and happiness and love. He wished—

The sound of wheels crunching over gravel in the alleyway caused him to freeze where he stood.

"I thought you said all the guests had already arrived, and none would leave for hours," Bianca murmured against Harry's lips.

That *was* what he had said. Everyone who intended to come would have arrived well before supper was served. And with the spectacular display of meteors shooting overhead, no guest in their right mind would choose this moment to summon their carriage to take them home.

Which meant it could only be... a guest *not* in their right mind.

Harry lifted his mouth from Bianca's and stepped in front of her protectively just as a familiar voice slurred out of the open hackney window, "Son? Is that you?"

"You've missed supper, Father," Harry replied evenly. "You ought to continue on home."

The hackney's passenger door flung open even

before the wheels fully came to a stop. "What are you doing out here, if the party is in there?"

"Everyone stepped outside to see the shooting stars," Harry explained, then wished he hadn't.

Father immediately lurched out of the hackney, stumbling as his boots hit the rocks, an almost-empty bottle of the Savoy Club's port dangling from his hand.

He squinted up at the sky and grunted. "Too blurry. They don't hold still."

"Get back into the carriage," Harry coaxed. "Have the driver take you home."

God help him if his father insisted on marching drunkenly into the St. Trevelyons' rear garden and vomited in front of all the guests. Then there would be no Lady Regina or *any* heiress to save them.

Father spun tipsily and turned his squinting gaze on Harry. "What's that behind you?"

"Not a what. A who. And never mind that right now. Just get in the carriage and—"

"Is that *Quinseley's* by-blow? It is, isn't it! I may be drunk, but I'm not stupid. She's got that same unfortunate patch of white at her temple."

"I'm sorry about this," Harry murmured to Bianca, then took a step aside in order to make proper introductions. "Father, this is Miss Bianca White. Miss White, this is my—"

"Yes, yes," Father slurred, "That's what I said, didn't I? I can see who it is. What I want to know is what the devil you think you're doing with her. And don't say you weren't kissing her, because I could

122

see that you were. I gave you explicit instructions—"

Harry gritted his teeth as his father waxed on drunkenly about refilling coffers and the monetary value of heiresses and sons who should be fulfilling their destiny, not wasting time with meaningless flirtations.

If anyone else had caught them in a scandalous embrace—or, perhaps, if *Bianca* were anyone else— their kiss would be considered a "compromise". As a gentleman, Harry would be forced to marry Bianca to preserve her honor.

But because his father could not see beyond their empty bank account, and because Bianca was born on the wrong side of the blanket, there would be no worse consequences than an inebriated tongue-lashing from a man who had given up on standing upright and had now seated himself in the open doorway of the hackney carriage, right where countless muddy boots had passed.

"I'm sorry," Harry said again to Bianca. "Go back the way we came and find your friends. With luck, everyone's attention will still be on the sky, and no one will think to wonder where you might have wandered off to all alone."

Bianca cast a dubious look at Harry's father, then nodded and hurried off into the shadows.

"And furthermore—" slurred the marquess, shaking his almost-empty bottle of port for emphasis.

"Get in the carriage at once," Harry commanded,

using the stern-headmaster voice he'd learned at a young age was the only tone his intoxicated father would respond to.

Father glowered at him without pausing his own rant for more than a hiccup, but stood obediently and managed to climb back into the hackney.

"Stay here inside the carriage," Harry ordered. "I'll go and fetch Tina."

"Is the ball over?" Father said in surprise.

"Yes." It was now. For Harry and Tina both. But it was better for the festivities to be cut short rather than for their lives to be ruined by the marquess thundering into their midst, drinking straight from the bottle.

"Never mind Christina." Father took another swig of his port. "Go after Lady Regina. You've got big money on the line, son. Reel it in."

"I'll try my best," Harry said, "if you promise to stay here until I return."

The marquess looked about in surprise, as if hadn't noticed he was in a hackney until just this moment. "Whose carriage is this? Yours?"

Grimly, Harry turned to the hackney driver. "Don't let him out of your sight."

CHAPTER 17

"**B**ut why do *I* have to go home early?" grumbled Tina, shocking Harry as he helped her into the hackney carriage. His shy sister never wanted to remain at a crowded society event a minute longer than absolutely necessary.

Part of him was tempted to answer, *Because we don't have enough blunt for two hackneys*, but Harry held his tongue. The horrid state of the family's finances were neither Tina's fault, nor her responsibility to fix. Harry tried to shield her as much as possible from the true depths of their father's excesses.

"Caught your brother seducing that orphan with the white hair," slurred the marquess.

"Bianca?" Tina swung her gaze toward Harry as he climbed into the rear-facing seat and tapped on the panel to set the driver in motion. "You've never been *caught* before. Isn't that grounds for compromise? Are there wedding bells in your future?"

"There had better be," said Father. "With that Lady Regina."

Tina frowned. "You *didn't* compromise Bianca?"

Father waved his bottle. "Nobody saw."

"*You* saw."

"I told him to drop the baggage and go after the purse."

"Lovely." Her gaze cut to Harry. "Is this your plan as well?"

"It's complicated," he hedged.

"It's not complicated. It's a rule that literally everyone knows: if a gentleman is caught in a compromising position with a lady, he must marry her."

"Exactly," said Father. "He *ought* to have seduced Lady Regina."

"Did you lure Bianca out-of-doors expressly because you had no intention of behaving honorably toward her?" Tina demanded.

"I had already warned her I would not be offering marriage." Harry's words sounded defensive even to his own ears. "I am a known rake. She was not expecting me to behave otherwise. But no, I didn't plan to seduce her. I... "

Had already told her I was turning over a new leaf. That I was rehabilitating my reputation. That I would behave like a gentleman from now on.

Harry frowned. *Had* Bianca thought his earlier

warning of ungentlemanly intentions no longer held true?

"I told her not to trust you," Tina muttered.

"She's not ruined," Harry protested. "No one saw anything but Father, and he's hardly the world's most reliable witness."

The marquess was too busy coaxing the last few drops of port from his bottle to respond to this.

Tina sniffed and crossed her arms.

"It was just a kiss," Harry tried again. "We were caught up in the moment. It will likely never happen again."

"It had better not." Father flung his empty bottle to the floor and shoved his hand deep into his pocket, squirming against the squab as he reached for some hidden item. He brought his hand down on Harry's with satisfaction. "*There*. That's what you need."

Harry stared down at the thin gold band now laying in his palm. "Is this Mother's wedding ring?"

Father nodded. "From my marchioness to yours."

"I thought Mother was buried with her ring."

"I took it off her hand at the funeral." The marquess folded Harry's fingers over the ring. "Don't be so missish. Your mother's dead. What use has she for jewelry now? Give that bauble to your Lady Regina. You weren't going to buy a ring for her any other way."

That was... extremely unsentimental, and unfortunately true.

Harry wished he didn't feel like a lad being given a penny to purchase his own purgative. The situation certainly made him feel like vomiting.

There was only one woman he was interested in, and it wasn't Lady Regina. Earlier at the ball, during the set he'd shared with Regina, Harry had been forced to agree with—or rather, grind his teeth in silence through—a horrific number of disparaging comments about Bianca and virtually every other woman at the ball.

The more Lady Regina had talked, the worse Harry had felt for not speaking up in Bianca's defense, or on behalf of the other debutantes, but he couldn't risk Lady Regina deciding she and the Earl of Eagleton did not suit.

The fact that *Harry* had determined he and Lady Regina did not suit was neither here nor there. The whole family was counting on that dowry.

Harry had cautioned himself not to fall for any woman who wasn't an heiress. Feelings made everything more complicated. Once the heart was involved, Harry's only choices were to fail himself or to fail his family.

He uncurled his fingers and stared down at his mother's old wedding ring. Father might be a drunk, but he wasn't wrong. The only path forward was to put this ring on Lady Regina's finger.

And to do so, Harry would have to keep playing the gentleman. Regina's interest in him was because of his title, but there were other men with titles. The reason she was considering his suit was because of his comparatively young age to the other titled bachelors, and because he'd spent the past fortnight doing his best to prove he was no longer the feckless rake he once was.

The mission was so successful, people had started calling him Eagleton again, instead of the Huntsman. Lady Regina's brother, the Duke of Lennox, had even inclined his head to Harry when he'd come to collect the duke's sister for their set, giving his tacit approval to the match.

"So what's taking so long?" slurred Harry's father.

"I can't propose to her right now," Harry muttered. "She's at a ball and we're in a hackney carriage."

"I can't believe you're really going to propose to Lady Regina." Tina shook her head in disgust. "I could make a long list of marriageable young women better than her."

"A dowry by any other name would not smell as sweet," said Father.

Harry tried to act as though their union wouldn't be completely miserable. "It's not so bad. She's young, pretty, accomplished, clever… "

"*Rich*," Father added.

And perhaps most importantly, willing and eager to make a coldhearted trade: a title for a dowry.

Tina wrinkled her nose. "And Bianca? Is she none of those things?"

"She's… " Young. Pretty. Accomplished. Clever.

"Not rich," Father said flatly. "Or a lady."

Harry cut him an irritated look. "You said yourself that being a lady was the least of our concerns. There was that textiles heiress you thought would make a fine—"

"Pah." Father flapped his hand in dismissal. "You settle when you *have* to settle. But now there's no need. Not when you can have the best of both worlds. Besides, even if that orphan had a dowry—"

"That orphan has a *name*. 'Miss White.' I introduced you."

Tina's eyes widened. "You paused your seduction to make proper introductions?"

"Even if she had a dowry," the marquess continued unrepentantly. "You're dodging a bullet."

Harry didn't feel as though he were dodging a bullet. He felt like he'd been struck with an arrow. Cupid's, specifically.

With Bianca, he shared more than ordinary passion. Much as Harry hated to admit it, he was emotionally invested. His feelings for her went well beyond the physical. He wanted her in his bed, in his home, in his life. Not for one night, but all of them.

It was enough to tempt a man to give up on dowries, and take a chance on his heart instead.

"How about you?" Harry nudged Tina's slipper. "When are you tying the knot?"

She sent him a withering look. "I can't even get signatures on my dance card."

"I could help you to become less shy. We could practice conversations and improvise various scenarios until you feel more comfortable around gentle—"

"My blank dance card isn't because I'm *shy*," Tina ground out with obvious disbelief. "It's because I don't have a *dowry*. Lords like you would dance attendance on a dry log if it came with enough gold. I'm not worth the effort."

Harry's stomach hollowed as he stared back at Tina in dawning horror. His brain was sluggish to process that his bashful little sister was not actually timid. She simply believed no one would ever want her for herself. Why bother acting out a futile role, and building her hopes up for nothing?

Tina's biting appraisal of "men like him" stung. In no small part, because it had rung true up until he'd met Bianca... and was going to have to become true once again.

If Harry had married an heiress sooner, Tina could have had a dowry in time for her come-out. She might never have been relegated to the wallflowers if he had done his duty the moment he realized the dire straits his family was in, instead of dragging his feet in the hopes of encountering an heiress with whom he *suited*.

Harry didn't need to suit. He needed to provide for his sister. If one of the siblings deserved a love match, it was sweet Tina, not selfish Harry.

She was counting on him, and he knew just what

to do. After all, he was the Huntsman, was he not? A coldhearted fortune-hunter with a fresh fish on the line. If marrying a woman with piles of money was the sacrifice he needed to make for his family, he would need to stop dallying and do it.

Even if it meant walking away from Bianca.

CHAPTER 18

*B*ianca tried to pay close attention to the playing cards in her hands, truly she did, but she couldn't help but hope Harry would wander into the sitting room at any moment.

She and Tina were seated across from each other at a tea table devoid of any tea, playing their third round of Casino in a row. As an only child, Bianca had not had much opportunity to play cards growing up, but Tina was a splendid instructor. She won every hand, explaining exactly how she did it as she went along, so that Bianca would not fall for the same tricks a second time.

In theory, anyway. The thing was, Bianca hadn't had a moment alone with Harry since the kiss they'd shared beneath the shooting stars. The last time Bianca had been to Tina's house, Harry had accompanied Bianca out in the rain to flag a hackney carriage. Today, the sky was stubbornly blue, but she could not help but hope Harry would step out of the shadows as he'd done the time before and claim a moment of her time.

Which Bianca planned to spend with their lips locked in another kiss.

"No," Tina said patiently. "I don't recommend that combination. Let me see your hand."

Bianca displayed her cards obediently and played the ones Tina suggested.

The reason Bianca could not get Harry out of her mind was not because they'd shared a scandalous kiss. As the daughter of a courtesan, Bianca wasn't the least concerned about Polite Society's rules of propriety. If she wanted to indulge in a kiss, she would do so without hesitation or self-recrimination. If Bianca wished to take a lover, then she'd do that, too.

What she wanted to know was if it had *meant* something to Harry, other than yet one more stolen kiss in a rakish lifetime of stolen kisses.

The problem was, it hadn't been "just a kiss" for Bianca. She could line up every other gentleman in that ballroom and kiss them all night long without feeling the slightest spark. With Harry, it was more than a spark. It was an inferno. An eternal flame that burned deep within her soul.

She didn't want to put out the fire. She wanted to fan the flames higher. She wanted him to burn for her as she burned for him. But only the foolish believed wishes came true.

Bianca had hoped he would come to call.

He hadn't.

She had hoped he would barge into the sitting room where she sat with his sister, using any nonsensical pretext that came to mind as an excuse to see Bianca again, if only for a moment, across a room.

He hadn't.

If Harry did not care about her, if they were not to be friends or lovers or anything else, she could make her peace with that. But to do so, first she needed to know the truth. *Was* she nothing more than a conquest? Or, when he kissed her, had he also felt—

Footsteps sounded out in the corridor.

Bianca froze, her white-knuckled fingers denting the cards as she cocked her ear toward the open doorway and listened with all her might.

The steps paused, just outside the visible section of the corridor, as if whoever stood there was listening just as intently, whilst deciding whether or not to make their presence known. After a long, interminable moment, a soft sigh sounded, and the footsteps retreated from the sitting room.

Bianca dropped her cards and sprang to her feet. "I'll be right back. I have to... I have to visit the water closet."

She hurried from the room without glancing to see whether Tina was remotely fooled by this thin excuse.

Bianca had barely taken three steps down the corridor when the figure at the other end turned around.

It *was* Harry! Bianca's breath caught and her skin flushed hot.

He was gorgeous as always, but in a different way than before: Bianca had caught him in deshabille. Rather than his rakish ballroom uniform of black breeches and black tailcoat, with a perfectly starched white cravat at his throat, Harry's strong legs were encased in soft buckskins, and his shoulders unfettered by any coat. A smart waistcoat of wine and taupe complemented the buckskins, but his shirtsleeves fluttered free in the invisible breeze of an open window.

If she touched his arms now, the way that she had that starry, starry night, she would be able to feel his musculature and his warmth through the thin linen that cloaked him.

Harry did not come to her. Nor did he turn away. He stood there helplessly, staring back at her with unconcealed hunger, his posture tensed as though poised to flee but unable to move an inch.

It was as though their roles had been reversed. She was now the huntress, and he the prey. A sense of power infused her blood and quickened her heartbeat.

Very well. She was no frightened rabbit. If it was up to her to make the conquest, then conquer she would.

She took a step forward, then another, then another. Harry remained still as a statue—or still as a deer startled in the forest—but he drank her in as though his thirst for her would never be sated.

Good. Bianca felt the same way. The sight of him did not quench her desire, but rather made her hunger for him all the more.

When she reached him, she kept her voice coy, light. "Weren't you going to greet your guest, my lord?"

"No," he said hoarsely, unable to take his gaze from her.

She reached out to touch his chest, then paused with her fingertip half an inch above the loose V of his neckline. Close enough to sense his warmth and feel the air pulse with each beat of his heart.

"I suppose I should leave you alone, if I'm unwanted," she murmured.

Before she could lower her arm, he grabbed her around the waist and whirled her up against the wall. Her spine flattened against the silk wall coverings. She barely had time to gasp aloud before he slanted his mouth over hers, claiming her in a kiss.

She met him just as hungrily. He laced his fingers with hers, trapping the backs of her hands up against the silk of the wallpaper, high above either side of her head. His body covered hers, big and hard and hot, pressing against her as though they were seconds away from making love right here in the corridor.

And it *would* be love, damn him. As much as Bianca tried not to admit it, her feelings for him were nothing so simple as mere lust. She wanted to writhe in his arms and then sleep nestled against his chest. She wanted to share the marmalade with him at breakfast and pour his tea at nuncheon. She wanted—

He tore his mouth from hers, panting. "*No*. I can't."

"Can't what? Kiss me? You were doing a mighty fine job."

"Can't hurt you." He touched his forehead to hers.

She frowned. "It didn't hurt."

"It will." He dropped her hands abruptly and stepped back, raking a hand through his wavy ginger hair. "That must be our last kiss, Bianca. I told you, I cannot marry you."

"I didn't ask for marriage." But that was what she wanted, wasn't it? The marmalade, the tea, the cozy nights before a fire. She didn't want to be Harry's secret mistress. She wanted to be his wife.

"You didn't ask for any of this. Neither did I. And yet…" He rubbed a hand over his face, then visibly forced himself to meet her eyes. "I'm going to marry Lady Regina."

CHAPTER 19

*B*ianca stared at Harry with her heart in her throat. Of all the women he could marry, if it couldn't be her... Why did it have to be the insufferable Lady Regina?

Tina's voice came from down the corridor. "Bianca?"

As she whirled around to face her friend, Bianca did her best to paste a smile on her face.

Tina did not look convinced. "Are you all right?"

Bianca glanced over her shoulder. Harry was gone. She was alone.

And it seemed she would stay that way.

"I'm fine," she lied.

Tina walked up to join her. "What did he do?"

"Who?" Bianca stammered. "I just... The water closet... "

Tina gestured over her shoulder. "The water closet is in the opposite direction."

Bianca sighed and rubbed her temples. "He says he's marrying Lady Regina."

Tina did not look surprised. Only sympathetic. "Father is forcing him to."

Bianca scoffed. "How can your father force Harry to do anything? He's a grown man, and he'll inherit the marquessate regardless of his father's wishes."

"He'll also inherit generations of debt. Unless he marries an heiress. Trust me, he'd rather hurl himself from the cliffs of Dover." Tina shrugged, as if this were the most obvious and ordinary consideration to make when selecting a bride.

Bianca stared at her. "Harry doesn't even like Lady Regina?"

"He can't stand her. It's probably mutual. She wants his title and the right to boast about taming the notorious Huntsman. He wants her dowry. Polite Society considers that a fair trade."

"He doesn't even like Lady Regina," Bianca repeated. She wasn't sure if that made the situation better or worse. Perhaps a little of both.

Tina lifted a shoulder apologetically. "We need money. She has it. Her parents are almost as wealthy as yours were."

"My mother didn't—"

"Sorry, I meant your father. The Earl of Quinseley had more money than God, according to... well, everyone."

"And now Lady Quinseley has it," Bianca said with a sigh. If only there had been some cousin or nephew to inherit the earldom! Perhaps the current circumstances would be different. "Why do the worst people get rewarded for being the worst people?"

Before Tina could answer—if indeed a satisfactory explanation existed for the question posed—the knocker banged a familiar pattern against the town house's front door.

"It's the others!" Tina hurried toward the entrance. "What are they doing here?"

Bianca and Tina arrived just as the butler swung open the door, allowing a wave of wallflowers to spill into the entranceway.

"Grab your bonnets, ladies," Joy sang out sunnily. "We're going to Hyde Park!"

"We are?" Tina said doubtfully. "We never go to Hyde Park."

"Today we are," said Goose. "We're celebrating!"

Tina accepted her bonnet from the butler. "What are we celebrating?"

Goose clapped her hands. "It's Bianca's birthday in two days, and we have the best present. She—"

Peavy clapped a hand over Goose's mouth. "Don't spill the secret yet."

"Are you certain I'm fancy enough to mingle with aristocrats and the fashionable?" Bianca asked as she tied on her bonnet.

"More than fancy enough," Doc said confidently.

"Come on, come on!" Bouncing on her toes, Joy ushered the group out of the town house and into a large coach-and-four, where they nonetheless had to squeeze their hips together and sit on each other's laps in order to fit eight women in a single carriage.

Luckily, the entrance to the park was less than a mile from the Eagleton town house.

Every afternoon at this hour, the cream of Polite Society gathered in Hyde Park to gad about in long, looping circles for two hours a day. The more raffish gentlemen were astride horses or atop rackety phaetons. The more stately ladies were ferried about in open barouches and landaus. Everyone else strolled on foot—all the better to see and be seen.

"Let's promenade!" said Joy as the eight friends tumbled out of the overstuffed carriage.

The young women linked arms in two rows of four and set off on the footpath.

"What's this about?" Bianca asked Joy as the group found its rhythm.

Tina was on Bianca's other side, and Peavy was on Joy's other arm.

Joy looked as though she might explode with happiness. "You remember how Peavy's father is a solicitor?"

"Yes," Bianca answered warily. "Am I going to have to defend myself to a judge for my birthday?"

"That's what a barrister does, not a solicitor," Tina whispered.

Joy squeezed Bianca's arm. "Peavy mentioned to her parents that you had attended the St. Trevelyan ball with us. And do you know what her father replied?"

"Of course she doesn't know," said Tina. "We weren't there."

"Joy, just *tell* her," interjected Peavy.

"All right, all right." Joy's eyes sparkled. "Peavy's father said, 'I'll wager the poor girl never has a moment to sit down, with a dowry like hers.'"

Bianca blinked. "He said what?"

"You have a dowry," Joy said, bubbling over with excitement.

"I... have a dowry?" Bianca said faintly.

"A big one," Peavy confirmed. "Father was the solicitor who wrote it up. He can't recall the terms precisely because it's been twenty years since last he saw them—"

"My father provided a dowry for me when I was a *baby*?" Bianca stared at Peavy in confusion and wonder. "Why wouldn't he have mentioned this?"

"Mother says the earl wanted you to find a love match. She reminded Father that he wasn't supposed to *tell* people about your dowry, because Quinseley was so certain you wouldn't need one. It was to be a wedding gift for the man who won your heart."

"But... but... " Bianca could think of no coherent words. "Then what are we doing *here*?"

"We're going to tell *everyone*!" Joy blurted out in excitement. "There's no need to wait for Peavy's father to rummage up an old copy of the terms.

You're an *heiress*, Bianca. They cannot ignore you now."

Bianca glanced over her shoulder at the others. "Are you all hearing this?"

They were gone. Doc and Goose and Rosie and Miss Drowsy had scattered to the four winds, each spreading the delicious gossip of Bianca's staggering dowry among the crowd like dandelion seeds scattering in the wind.

In no time, Bianca was beset by fashionable gentlemen dropping by to bid a good afternoon to Joy or Tina or Peavy, and… What's this? A friend of yours? Do be so kind as to make an introduction. Oh, Miss White! The pleasure is all mine! Might I call upon you tomorrow?

Bianca's head spun. Not just because of all the unexpected attention, but because of what the dowry would mean. Bianca needn't spend the rest of her life as a maid-of-all-work, or an indigent burden camped in her friends' guest rooms.

All she had to do was marry, and a large chunk of her father's riches would be hers.

Technically, the money would belong to Bianca's future husband. As would Bianca herself. But she would be twenty-one in two days. Once she had her majority, she could decide her future for herself. No one could force her into a loveless marriage. There would be no walking down the aisle unless she chose to do so of her own free will.

Unfortunately, the one man she'd hoped would choose *her…* had already chosen someone else.

CHAPTER 20

*H*arry tried and failed to keep his focus on the charts of accounts lying open on the desk before him. In theory, all his worries would soon be over. He need only slip a ring on Lady Regina's finger… and then live with that decision for the rest of his life.

He couldn't even bring Lady Regina's face to mind. Every time he blinked, it was Bianca's countenance that filled the canvas of his memory. How fetching she looked, drugged with passion, kissing him.

How hurt she'd looked when he'd spurned her and walked away.

It had taken every ounce of his will not to run back to her arms, to throw himself at her feet, to beg her not to let a measly little unhappy loveless marriage come between them.

But Harry believed in marriage. In the idea of it, in the promise of loyalty and monogamy and forever. Even if Bianca was willing to be his mistress indefinitely, as her mother had been for Lord Quinseley, such an arrangement was not good enough for Harry.

It wasn't good enough for *Bianca*.

If he couldn't offer her all of him, then he had no business offering any part of himself at all.

Harry pushed away the ledger of accounts. He removed his mother's ring from his pocket and glared down at it with self-recrimination.

Wasn't the same true for Lady Regina? Did he have any business offering any part of himself, when he already knew she would never have his heart?

Or was this just another high-handed, Harry-knows-best line of reasoning?

An hour ago, he had asserted that as long as Lady Regina entered into the bargain with open eyes, and not only knew precisely what she was getting, but also was satisfied with the trade... Then no one had any right to stop them.

By his own logic, then, if Bianca knew all she would ever have of Harry was a stolen night here and there, and nonetheless was satisfied with such an arrangement, who was he to limit what sort of liaisons she could or could not have?

The fact was, it was Harry who did not wish to share. He wanted Bianca all to himself. And he did not want Lady Regina at all.

Yet he knew his duty. Family came first. Or rather, according to the British aristocracy, family came second and the title came first. But the family finances had not deteriorated to this point from his father's drinking habits alone. The marquess had inherited an already terrible situation from his own father, who likely had begun at a disadvantage from his as well.

One could regard such a history despondently... Or one could take a more hopeful interpretation, and conclude that even the worst offenders to mismanage the marquessate had not managed to ruin it. Father might have given up, but Harry had not. Marrying money was one way out of this hole, but who said it was the only way?

Perhaps Harry should start by questioning the assumption that living as lavish a life as the spend-thrift Prince Regent was even the goal to aspire to.

Bianca would never be fully accepted by all of Polite Society. If Harry chose her, he would be unceremoniously barred from Almack's. Was that so dreadful? Forgoing that subscription would save him ten guineas a year.

And then there was this town house. What a dreadful expense! The most fashionable neighborhood, a full battalion of servants. If he directed those funds toward the entailed estates instead, and rented a cheap room when Parliament was in session...

Well, he still wouldn't have enough money, but perhaps he could staunch the flow.

If they put their minds together—Harry, Bianca, Tina, even Father—perhaps they could find a financial solution that did not require decades of misery.

Carriage wheels crunched outside. Harry glanced out the open study window in time to see the Gladwells' coach-and-four roll to a halt in front of the house.

Quickly, Harry shoved the ring back into his pocket. He raced from the study and out through the front door to catch the carriage before it left with Bianca inside.

Tina was waving goodbye to her friends when he skidded out of the house.

"Miss White," he called out. "Could I speak with you for a moment?"

At first, he thought she would politely decline. But then she murmured something to her friends, who melted aside so that the footman could hand her down from the carriage.

Tina edged closer with avid interest.

"I'd like to speak with Miss White privately," he informed his sister pointedly.

She made a face, but then shrugged and went to talk to her friends while he had a moment alone with Bianca.

Semi-alone. They were standing next to an over-stuffed carriage on a busy street in the middle of Mayfair.

Harry would take what he could get.

"I'm sorry for earlier," he said quietly.

Bianca arched her brows. "You're sorry you ran away, or you're sorry you kissed me?"

"I will never regret any kiss shared with you. I will always regret causing you pain. The truth is—"

She placed her hand on his chest. "Spare me the excuses. I already know your stance and your reasons."

"I don't think you do." He caught her hand and held it against him.

Lightly, she tugged her fingers free. "I have had an unexpectedly eventful afternoon, and am looking forward to an evening alone with a good book. I hope you enjoy yours as well, however it is that you choose to do so."

"Most likely, also alone with a book," he said wryly. "Unless I can talk you into—"

"You can't. I'm busy."

"What about tomorrow?"

"Busy."

"The day after tomorrow?"

She shook her head. "It's a long book."

"It's also your birthday," he reminded her. "If you want to spend your birthday reading, then by all means, you should do so. But you'll also need to eat. Please allow me to spirit you away for a picnic. Even if all you have to spare is half an hour."

She arched a skeptical eyebrow. "Is this to be a chaperoned or unchaperoned picnic?"

He smiled. "Lady's choice."

She snorted. "I'll think about it."

Was it any wonder Harry loved her? He gave her his most rakish smile. "Is that a yes for the birthday picnic?"

She gave him a long look. "Any specific reason you changed your mind and are suddenly eager to break bread with me and two dozen friendly ants?"

"I enjoy spending time with you," he answered honestly. He slid his hand into his pocket and touched the ring with his fingertips. "I have a gift I hope you'll like."

"Hmm," was all she said before turning around and strolling back to the carriage.

"It's rude not to take your proper leave of someone," he called out.

"Bianca can do what she wants," piped up the one they called Goose. "She just found out she's—"

One of the others clapped a hand over Goose's mouth.

The carriage pulled away before Harry could ask any questions.

He turned to Tina instead. "What was that about?"

"Early birthday present," she answered. "Will you be going out tonight?"

"I won't be making any social appearances at all until I resolve our situation." He fingered the ring in his pocket. Was choosing love the right answer? "Also, I might have to literally hold Father down to prevent him from going out and incurring even more bills we cannot pay."

Tina brightened.

Harry narrowed his eyes with suspicion. "Why do you ask?"

"No reason," she said innocently. "Ignorance is bliss."

She skipped off into the town house before he could take her to task for whatever secret she was keeping from him.

Rather than follow his sister, Harry stared after the distantly retreating coach-and-four instead. He had a picnic to plan. A question to propose. A mission to achieve.

He would carry around this ring until Bianca agreed to become his wife.

CHAPTER 21

*A*n afternoon picnic in Richmond Park was perhaps not the night of champagne and opera that Harry wished he could give Bianca, but at least their surroundings were beautiful. Richmond Park was one of the largest in London. It contained many pedestrian walkways and acres of unexplored woods, home to countless deer and other animals.

The basket in Harry's arms contained food and drink and a large blanket. But arguably the most important element to keep track of was the engagement ring in his pocket.

"What, ho, Eagleton!" called out a jovial voice.

Harry wished he could pretend not to have heard. He was trying to stage a romantic birthday for Bianca, and the last thing he needed were old Oxford mates blathering about the weather or horse races or the new cut of their waistcoat.

"Good afternoon." Harry inclined his head to Lord Devin, hoping that would be the end of it.

It was not.

"You wily old goat," said Devin. He clapped Harry on the shoulder with a knowing look in his eye. "The Huntsman is a bloodhound, eh? Should've known you'd be the first to smell the scent of pounds sterling in the air."

Harry stared at him in confusion. "What?"

"Oh, don't get your cravat twisted, I'm only bamming with you. My felicitations, old man, honestly. I should've bet on you at White's. When are the nuptials, then?"

"We're not betrothed," Bianca said tightly.

"Oh." Lord Devin's startled gaze flew from Harry to Bianca and back again. "*Oh.*"

"No," Harry corrected quickly. "This is not a protector-and-mistress situation."

"Well… of course it isn't," Devin said uncertainly. "Why would *you* pay *her*, when *she's* the one with the money? A dowry like that would set a man up for life."

Harry blinked. "She has the *what* did you just say?"

"Oh, how horribly vulgar of me." Devin's face flushed red. "Of course we shouldn't talk about money. It's not even *my* money, and here I am nattering on as if it's any business of mine. I'm no better than a sewing circle with a pot of scandal broth. My apologies, Miss White. Whenever you do make your selection... My felicitations will still stand."

He hurried off down the walking path before Harry or Bianca could say a single word.

Harry turned to Bianca. "Do you have any notion what that cork-brain was... talking about... "

Bianca's expression was not confused, but guilty. As if she had been trying very hard to keep a secret and Devin had just let the cat out of the bag. A secret like...

"You have a *dowry*?" Harry said in disbelief.

Bianca made a chagrined little smile.

"A big one? A dowry of such mountainous proportions, awestruck lords stop you in the park to comment upon it?"

"'Big' is a relative term," she hedged.

"Well, is it bigger than everyone else's?" he sputtered.

She made a face, then nodded.

"Then it's objectively big, not relatively big. It's... How did you keep it a secret?"

"I didn't know until two days ago."

This was what Tina had been trying to keep from him. But why? Did she think it would change how Harry felt about Bianca?

Was that what *Bianca* thought?

"Why didn't you tell me?" he asked softly.

"I didn't want... " She gestured at him. "... *this* reaction."

The slender gold ring in his pocket felt like a

lump of lead. "You thought if you told me, I'd immediately offer marriage?"

She inclined her head. "It was a reasonable assumption."

Harry ground his teeth. It *was* a reasonable assumption, damn it. One that he could not defend himself from. He had never hid his aims as a fortune-hunter. If he asked Bianca to marry him now, why would she have any reason to believe the question motivated by love, and not by his empty pocketbook?

"I don't want to be wooed for my money," she said quietly. "Even by you."

Definitely not the moment to mention the ring in his pocket. Of all the infernal turns of events... Why couldn't Devin have held his fool tongue until *after* Harry had made his proposal?

Then again, would Bianca have believed Harry in ignorance about a dowry so large random park-goers recognized her on sight? Perhaps it was just as well that Lord Devin had spilled the beans. Harry was likely to only have one shot at crafting a winning proposal. It was better to know what he was up against than to scramble to fix an impression he hadn't known he was giving.

Oh, very well, an impression he'd crafted and espoused to anyone who would listen. He was called The Huntsman, not The Nice Gentleman Who Definitely Isn't After Your Dowry.

How the devil was he going to convince Bianca his feelings for her were sincere?

"Let's go this way," he said gruffly. "I scouted a clearing where we shouldn't be bothered."

"Mm-hm," she murmured. "A rake like you must have seduced a dozen women in your secluded clearing."

He cut her a sharp look.

She held up her palms and blinked wide eyes. "I don't mind in the least. In fact, my only birthday wish is to sow a few wild oats of my own."

Good God. How was Harry supposed to stay a gentleman when facing a request like *that*?

"Blast." She covered her mouth with her hands. "Goose told me my wishes won't come true if I say them aloud."

"I'd say your chances are still good," he muttered. "When it comes to seduction, letting your partner know what you want is the easiest way to ensure it happens."

She tilted her head. "But you didn't invite me here to seduce me, did you?"

"I told you." He set down the basket and shook out the blanket. "I'm on my best behavior."

"In a secluded clearing. With a woman you've exchanged torrid kisses with. And no chaperone."

"*My* best behavior, not a monk's best behavior," he grumbled.

"I'm not complaining," she assured him as she stretched out atop the blanket. "I'm just realizing... You really didn't know I was an heiress until Lord Devin mentioned the size of my dowry a few minutes ago."

He opened the wine and handed her a full glass. "I invited you here to celebrate your birthday."

"Nothing more and nothing less?"

He touched the pocket with the ring. "I might have hoped for a little something more."

Her eyes sparkled wickedly. "So might I."

Harry nearly choked on his wine.

Was Bianca seriously hoping for a seduction? Of course she was. If anyone knew her own mind on the subject, it would be the daughter of a courtesan. Her parents had been in love, and it hadn't been enough for Quinseley to be willing to marry her. If Bianca became intimate with Harry, it would be because she desired him, not because she thought it would be advantageous in any way. She fully expected him to ruin her and leave.

Or maybe she was the one willing to walk away. Perhaps Bianca believed the sparks between them would fizzle. That once they'd consummated their desire, they could go back to being casual acquaintances... or, worse, *strangers*. That after today, they need never see each other again.

It was up to Harry to change her mind.

CHAPTER 22

*B*ianca lay on her back atop the blanket, her bent knees aiming skyward beneath her ankle-length skirts.

The previous year at this time, she had spent her birthday cleaning the flues of Lady Quinseley's fireplaces. Today, she was surrounded by the calming sounds of nature in a picturesque secluded clearing. Instead of scrubbing bricks by herself, Bianca was relaxing in the company of a rakishly handsome lord whose attention had never once strayed from her face to take in the beauty of the trees and flowers surrounding them.

Nonetheless, the moment felt less like an overt seduction and more like a celebration. Harry's romantic picnic felt remarkably earnest. He had not brought her here to take advantage of her, but to make her happy.

Fortunately for them both, a birthday seduction would make Bianca very happy indeed. The connection they shared was palpable. Consummating their mutual desire could not make up for more than a year of abject loneliness, but would mark the perfect start of the next phase of her life. One with friends, with joy, and if all went well... with Harry.

He pulled fresh fruits from the basket. "Strawberry, madam?"

She opened her mouth obediently.

He brought the berries closer and stretched out beside her on the blanket, placing one of the fat red strawberries between her lips.

She bit into the berry. It was tart and sweet and perfect. The burst of juices filled her mouth with the flavor of springtime and happiness.

"Another?" Harry asked huskily.

She rolled onto her side and tipped her face up toward his. "Can you offer me something... more satisfying?"

He tossed the fruit back into the open basket and covered her mouth with his.

She wrapped her arms around his neck and pulled him to her. Their limbs tangled briefly in her skirts as his body aligned with hers. She ran her hands over his form. He felt divine beneath her palms, all warm planes and hard muscles.

Yet his mouth was sweet, soft, and gentle. As though he were wooing her with each kiss. Coaxing her onto a path she had already willingly taken. He wasn't leading her into a seduction. She was already there, pulling him along, taking them deeper.

"Do you know what I want for my birthday?" she murmured against his mouth. She felt his lips smile.

"A pony?"

"Close." She slid her finger beneath his cravat. "Though I'd prefer a different sort of ride."

He groaned and slanted his mouth over hers.

It wasn't quite a yes, but it also hadn't been a no. Bianca took heart. She well knew what she was asking. One could not grow up the daughter of a professional mistress without having learned a thing or two about the disposition and libidos of men, and the pleasures they could offer a woman.

Harry broke the kiss, panting. "I cannot take your virginity."

"You don't have to. I'm giving it up out of my own free will."

"What about… " He hesitated. "… your future husband?"

She rolled her eyes. "I'm definitely not saving my maidenhead for some greedy opportunist who wasn't interested in me until he learned of my dowry."

Harry winced.

She patted his cheek. "Don't you dare get offended by that phrasing. The Huntsman takes pride in being the ton's most infamous opportunist, does he not? You were also the first to give me a kind word, even when you thought me penniless."

"And your first kiss."

"And the second, and the third, and all the others. I've kissed no one but you. And in a few moments, I'll have made love to no one but you. That is, unless you'd rather I take these kisses to some *other* greedy opportunist eager to ensnare an heiress on her birthday…"

He claimed her mouth before she even finished talking.

Bianca was glad of it. He'd worried her for a moment. The unexpected dowry was both a blessing and a curse. She need no longer fear that she must live her life as an exhausted maid-of-all-work, sleeping four hours a night on a hard pallet only to push herself back up before sunrise to labor all over again.

But she was not free from worry altogether. The dowry was not hers to spend as she pleased. It would belong to her future husband, to use at his discretion. Just like Bianca would belong to her future husband, also to be used at his discretion. Money had a way of changing things—and people.

Was it any wonder Bianca wanted to know a moment's pleasure before committing herself to a lifetime of duty?

Besides, she knew from her mother that virginity—or its lack thereof—could not be determined by a groom on his wedding night. A bride might or might not have been born with an intact maidenhead, and any number of everyday activities, such as riding a horse, might have ruptured it since. Whether or not there was blood had more to do with the skill of the lover and his ability to arouse physical desire in his bride.

Why gamble on such vagaries of chance, when she could have the man of her choosing, right here and now?

Harry was more than a handsome rakehell. He had kissed her when he'd believed her an indigent runaway, thus proving his interest was not in her dowry. He had also *wanted* to kiss her, but refrained, when she was still a housemaid to Lady Quinseley— thus proving his honor. Harry wanted Bianca, but he would not take advantage when the power difference was in his favor.

He did not wish to *take* from her. Harry wished to *give* to her. He wanted every act to be caused by both of them equally, pleasuring them equally. He wanted both parties to enter into compromising positions willingly and eagerly, or not at all.

Bianca felt the same. She wanted her first love-making to be a moment that was shared, not one to be suffered through. She wanted it to be with a man who saw her as more than a purse. A man who saw her as a *person*. No matter her birth or upbringing or address.

She wanted it to be Harry.

Without taking his lips from hers, he tugged up the hems of her skirts, exposing her bare legs and hips to the copse of trees surrounding them. Bianca had only a moment to register the cool air from the spring breeze tickling across her skin before a new sensation enveloped her. She gasped into Harry's mouth as his hands explored and pleasured her body.

She supposed that, despite the precautions they'd taken to ensure privacy, there was always a chance that some other intrepid explorer would wander far off the marked paths and discover her here in Harry's arms.

Yet she could not make herself care.

What was the worst that could happen? Someone might say Harry was after her dowry. This wasn't news. Harry was after anyone and everyone's dowry.

Some might claim Bianca was following in her mother's footsteps, becoming mistress to an earl. This was ridiculous, given that Harry's empty coffers made it impossible for him to offer monetary recompense to any woman, courtesan or otherwise.

Others might call her ruined. Claim that no gentleman would have her now. But no gentleman had wanted her before. She'd been "ruined" when she'd swept the ashes from Lady Quinseley's fireplace. She'd been ruined when she was raised by a courtesan. She'd been ruined from the moment she'd been conceived, and born out of wedlock.

The size of her dowry meant there were men who would overlook such distasteful details.

Bianca didn't want to be overlooked. She wanted to be *seen*. She wanted to be kissed, and caressed, and loved. If only just long enough to make a memory to cherish for the rest of her life.

She arched in pleasure as Harry's skillful fingers brought her to heights she had only visited on her own before. This time was sweeter, more acute. Her body demanding and vulnerable all at the same time.

When he positioned his shaft at her entrance, his voice was ragged against her ear. "Stop me if you don't want this."

She wrapped her legs around him and tilted her hips up to meet him. "You're all that I want."

As they came together, he swallowed her soft gasp with a kiss. Soon she was climbing back up the precipice, but this time, with her hand in his, together. They soared higher and higher until the pressure was unbearable, then shattered as one into each other's arms.

Harry jerked out from her, spilling his seed across her thigh rather than risk what her father had done without thinking. He cleaned her skin with a handkerchief, then pulled her into his arms and cradled her close.

"Marry me," he murmured into her hair.

She chuckled. "I thought men were supposed to say whatever they thought women wanted to hear *before* taking their wicked way with them, not after."

"I'm in earnest."

"You're in recovery from intense physical activity. Give your brain a chance to start working again before you go making promises you won't want to keep."

"How can you think I don't want you?"

"Oh, I believe you *want* me. Just as you've seen that I want you. But I know you don't want to marry me. You showed no sign of it before. You're intoxicated by the after-glow of lovemaking."

"If you believe me temporarily addled, then I will pay a call on you in the morning to ask you again in the harsh light of day. Will that prove to you that my intentions are true?"

She nestled against his chest. "I suppose we'll find out tomorrow."

CHAPTER 23

*T*he next morning, breakfast came and went without any sign of Harry.

Bianca pretended she didn't care. She'd known from the beginning that she and the Earl of Eagleton were not destined for the altar. When they met, the first warning out of his mouth was that he would not offer marriage. Why *would* a lord offer for an illegitimate, impoverished chambermaid?

Of all the strikes against her, the only element that had changed was the reveal of her dowry. If he did appear at her door, would it be for Bianca, or for her dowry? Or for his guilty conscience at having taken her virginity?

Bianca scrubbed her face with her hands, then retrieved the stockings she'd been darning beside the fireplace. There was no hiding the truth, at least not from herself: She'd wanted to say *yes* right there on the picnic blanket, yesterday afternoon.

Until that moment, she'd thought lovemaking

the best possible birthday gift. But becoming Harry's countess would have outshone even that. Not because of the title, but because it would mean making love to each other on every future birthday, and all the nights in between.

But she hadn't wanted to trap him in a moment of misplaced guilt. If Harry was going to ask for her hand, she wanted him to mean it.

A distant knock sounded on the Gladwells' front door. The darning fell from Bianca's hands.

Harry had come, just as he'd said he would!

She leapt to her feet and took a step toward the door before turning right back around and retaking her seat on the sofa before the fire. She didn't want to seem overeager and desperate. It was better to await him here. The parlor was full of flowers from men whose marital enthusiasm had sparked the moment they'd learned of her dowry.

Harry was a fortune-hunter too, of that there was no doubt. But unlike all of these other gentlemen, Harry's interest in Bianca was genuine, and had been present from the start. If anyone deserved the dowry, it was him. He could save his family, just like he'd saved Bianca, and they would live happily ever—

Footsteps sounded in the corridor.

She scooped the discarded stockings up from the floor and feigned great interest in applying herself to darning a hole in the heel.

"Bianca?" came Goose's voice from the open doorway. "Your evil stepmother is here."

"I'm not her stepmother," Lady Quinseley snapped.

Bianca jerked her gaze up in surprise.

The countess stood at the entrance to the parlor with a lumpy burlap sack in her hands. She thrust the parcel at Goose. "Here. I found this pile of apples on your property."

Goose stared at the burlap sack, perplexed. "What am I supposed to do with them?"

"Take them," Lady Quinseley ground out, "to the kitchen."

Goose nodded and disappeared with the bag.

The countess tossed an apple to Bianca. "I saved the best one for you."

"You did?"

Bianca caught the blood-red apple in her skirts. It looked ripe and delicious. Perhaps she'd been wrong about Lady Quinseley. Or rather, perhaps her initial girlish hope of someday being friends had not been as foolish a dream as she had been led to believe.

She started to shine the apple on the muslin of her skirt.

"Don't rub it!" the countess commanded, then smiled. "It's already ready for you, dear."

Bianca set her darning aside and rose to her feet. "Should I ring for tea?"

"Oh, no, that won't be necessary. I cannot stay."

"Why have you come?" Perhaps to wish Bianca a belated birthday? Lady Quinseley had only missed it by a single day.

The countess's eyes glittered. "I have news I thought would be of interest."

"News of what?" Bianca's breath caught. "Has something happened to Harry?"

"Who? You cannot mean Eagleton. How would *I* know what that scheming fortune-hunter is up to? He says one thing and does the opposite. You should do well to forget him."

Bianca swallowed. Was that what had happened? Harry had said one thing, but would do the opposite? Was even her dowry not enough to tempt the Huntsman into wedlock?

"Then why have you—" she began.

Before she could finish the question, noise spilled out from the far end of the corridor. Mr. Gladwell had been enjoying a glass of sherry and a game of cards with Mr. Somers, Peavy's father. He and Mr. Gladwell were good friends.

As the men approached, Lady Quinseley tossed an icy blond ringlet over her shoulder.

"Well, isn't this a happy accident?" she cooed in a voice Bianca had never heard her use before.

"Lady Quinseley," Mr. Gladwell said stiffly. "Does my wife know you're here?"

"I'm afraid she's out, and I've missed her," Lady Quinseley replied in a tone that indicated she rarely missed anything at all. "Besides, I wasn't speaking to you. I was talking to Mr. Somers."

"Me?" the solicitor said in surprise. "We haven't seen each other in decades."

"Good heavens, don't make me sound *old*," the

countess scolded him. "Then again, I should like to rely on your memory."

Mr. Somers narrowed his gaze. "What's this about?"

"Our dear Miss White, of course." Lady Quinseley held her long fingers out toward Bianca. "She thinks she's an heiress."

Bianca frowned. "I *am* an heiress."

"You *were* an heiress," the countess corrected her with another ingratiating smile. "I thought you'd like to know that your status reverted to nothing at all on your birthday."

"W-what?" Bianca stammered. She had *just* learnt of the dowry. It couldn't be gone already!

"If you don't believe me, ask our friend Mr. Somers." Lady Quinseley crossed her arms under her bodice and gave the solicitor a pert look. "He's the one who drew up the contract."

"Years ago." Mr. Somers ran a hand through his thinning hair. "I haven't seen a copy of it since Miss White was a baby, but now that you mention it... I do recall a clause having to do with her twenty-first year. If memory serves, the earl made the dowry expire on that date to encourage Miss White to choose a husband sooner rather than later."

"But I've just found out about it this week," Bianca protested, her heart beating far too rapidly.

"Tut-tut." Lady Quinseley brushed her hands as if wiping away stray crumbs. "A contract is a contract. According to the terms set out by your own father, if you fail to wed by age one-and-twenty, the dowry funds revert to me."

"Actually," said Mr. Somers, "the dowry trust did not mention you. In the event Miss White remained unwed, the funds were to return to Lord Quinseley's personal accounts—"

"And he's dead," snapped the countess, "so the money belongs to *me*."

Mr. Somers swung his sympathetic gaze toward Bianca. "I'm sorry, child. Your father loved you more than life, and was certain you would wed your very first season, at sixteen. He'd thought to make the deadline age eighteen, but I talked him into twenty-one, so that you would at least have your majority."

"And that's all you have," Lady Quinseley said, her voice sickeningly sweet. "You're of age and out of my hair. Perhaps the Gladwells will shelter you for a little while, but once news leaks that you no longer possess a dowry... " The countess made an apologetic little shrug. "Who would want to marry you then?"

CHAPTER 24

*H*arry nervously fingered the gold wedding ring in his hand.

"I wish you'd have let me come by myself," he muttered beneath his breath.

His sister heard him anyway.

"I want to be the first to give Bianca a hug," Tina told him for the third time.

"What about me?" he protested.

"She'll hug you second," Tina promised.

"No hugs for me from my baby sister?" he teased.

She considered him with a far more serious look than he'd anticipated.

"For years," she said slowly, "I thought you nothing more than a ne'er-do-well."

"I didn't do much to counteract that image," he admitted.

"You cultivated it," she corrected him. "Everyone believed it. *I* believed it. And then came Bianca. You had every reason to walk away, based on the persona you portrayed, but you held your hand out to her instead."

"And now I've come to ask for *her* hand."

"If she'll have you, then I suppose you cannot be all bad," Tina allowed.

"What do you mean, '*if*' she'll have me, poppet?" Harry growled, stretching out the hand without the ring to tickle his sister.

Before he could make contact, the hackney door opened and Tina leapt out. "We're here!"

"At least let me be the one to knock on the door for my own proposal," he grumbled.

This wish was not to be granted.

As Harry and Tina strode up to the Gladwells' tidy cottage, the front door opened. Lady Quinseley stepped out, followed by the solicitor Mr. Somers.

"Now *there's* an odd couple," Tina murmured.

Harry could not help but agree. "What in the devil?"

Bianca appeared in the doorway, apparently to bid her visitors farewell. She did not look pleased to see them go. If anything, her color had drained, leaving her waxy and unnaturally pale. Her thin fingers curled around a dark apple the color of a fresh scab.

Upon sight of Harry, Lady Quinseley's eyes brightened, which chilled him to his bones.

"Lord Eagleton," drawled the countess, her icy blue eyes sparkling like shards of glass. "What a coincidence that *you* should come to call. I do hope my presence isn't interrupting anything... important."

Harry narrowed his eyes. Knowing Lady Quinseley, she'd planned every single aspect of this moment, including timing her exit to coincide with his arrival, just so she could say something to unsettle him right before he proposed to Bianca.

"Good day, Lady Quinseley," he said pointedly, stepping aside with a grand sweeping motion indicating she should pass on by. "Please, don't let me keep you."

She planted her feet where they were. "Perhaps I have a second or two I might spare. Don't let me stop you. What are you here for, *Huntsman*?"

Bianca closed her eyes as if in pain.

"No business of yours," Harry informed the countess. "Carry on, then. Back to your cauldron you go."

She smiled as if she merely found him amusing. "Lizard's leg and owlet's wing."

He stared at her. "What did you say?"

"It's Shakespeare," Tina whispered, behind him. "The next line is, 'For a charm of powerful trouble, like a hell-broth boil and bubble.' She's up to something."

"Of course she is up to something," he whispered back. "It's Lady Quinseley. With or without the theatrics, everything she does is a means to an end."

And she did not appear to be going anywhere any time soon.

Bianca sucked in a deep breath, then met his eyes. "Just say it. Then we can be done."

He frowned at her phrasing.

"That doesn't sound very romantic," he teased, trying to lighten the odd atmosphere. This was not how he had wanted his proposal to go. But if it was to be his only opportunity to ask the question he'd come for… He pulled the ring from his pocket and dropped to one knee. "My darling Bianca—"

"Good God, not *that* ring, I should hope," Lady Quinseley stage-whispered. "That ring was intended for Lady Regina."

Harry glared at the countess. "If you insist on being present when you are not wanted, at least have the decency to shut your mouth while you eavesdrop on a private conversation that has nothing to do with you."

"By all means." Lady Quinseley motioned him ahead. "I cannot wait to see how this ends."

"A new *beginning*," Harry said firmly, keeping his gaze locked on Bianca. "One in which you and I—"

"No," she said dully.

He blinked. "I haven't even got to the part where I—"

"No, I won't marry you."

"She's saving face," said the countess conspiratorially. "An admirable strategy. Choosing to reject you, before you can reject her."

"I haven't been carrying this ring around all week because I planned to *reject* her," he snapped.

"Of course not," Lady Quinseley agreed. "You've

been carrying it around because you planned to marry any vulgar chit with a dowry."

He gritted his teeth. "She is not a—"

"There's no dowry," Bianca cut in.

Harry recoiled and nearly toppled over. He tried to recover his balance and hide his shock, but it was too late. Bianca had seen his reaction.

Everyone had.

"Then it is true?" Her voice was hollow. "You don't want to marry *me*. You just wanted my dowry all along."

"Well, he certainly wasn't going to marry you for your *looks*," said Lady Quinseley. "At the St. Trevelyon crush, I overheard Lady Regina tell Eagleton that seeing a whore's by-blow in a ball gown was no better than putting cosmetics on a pig. And do you know what Eagleton said in response?"

Harry lowered the hand with the ring.

Bianca kept her eyes on his face. "What did he say?"

Lady Quinseley made a crocodile smile. "He said, 'Let's not waste breath talking about *her*. *Your* dance card says it is my turn to have a set with the prettiest young lady of them all.'"

Bianca nodded slowly, as if this was no less than what she'd expected. "I see."

Tina glared at him as though ready to run him through with a branch from the closest tree.

Harry had no defense. He'd said those words because he had just been threatened by his father. *Marry Lady Regina or our family is ruined.* Harry had spent all month staring at unpaid accounts that would never balance without immediate and drastic action.

Of *course* he would rather have married Bianca. But love did not pay the bills.

"Such chivalry," Tina hissed in disgust. "You are a prince among men."

"I knew what he was from the start," said Bianca. "I just wasn't wise enough to take him at his word."

"Oh, *have* you always known?" Lady Quinseley asked with faux innocence. "I didn't think he would have the gall to tell you that he accepted money in exchange for ruining you."

Bianca gasped.

Harry leapt to his feet and jabbed an angry finger toward the countess. "You're the one who—"

But Lady Quinseley wasn't looking at him. Her expression of delight centered straight on Bianca.

"You did do it!" the countess crowed in rapture. "You seduced her just as you said you would. Well done, lad. Now you've both lived up to my low expectations."

"Get out." Bianca's words came out garbled, as if strangled in her throat. "*Go.* All of you."

Harry spun toward her in desperation. "If you would just let me expl—"

Bianca took a loud, crunchy bite of the apple in her hand and slammed the door in his face.

Lady Quinseley clapped her hands in satisfaction and strolled to her waiting coach-and-four, cackling all the way.

Mr. Somers, who had watched the drama unfold in silence and disbelief, edged backward toward the open road.

Harry squared his shoulders and raised his hand to bang on the knocker.

Tina interposed herself between his arm and the front door.

"Stay away from her," she snapped.

He let out a frustrated breath. "Tina… "

"No. I'm done listening to you. Stay away from Bianca and stay out of my life, too."

CHAPTER 25

ith a final smirk out her window at Harry, Lady Quinseley rode off in her coach-and-four, her mission more than accomplished.

Harry glared after her, but in truth he was as angry with himself as he was with the countess. She had come to the Gladwells with the intent to shatter dreams, and had succeeded.

But she hadn't lied. She hadn't needed to.

It was not Lady Quinseley's fault that her dearly departed husband's arrogant conviction that his illegitimate daughter would wed within months of her come-out had spurred the earl to add an ill-advised end date on Bianca's dowry.

Nor was Lady Quinseley to blame for Harry accepting her devil's bargain to ruin Bianca in exchange for a few quid. At the eleventh hour, he'd shown some mettle and refused to go through with the plot, sending Bianca off to safety instead... Only to end up in a woodsy clearing a fortnight later, doing exactly the thing he'd sworn he wouldn't do.

"I'll flag a hackney," Tina said without looking at him. "Two hackneys."

"We can't afford two hackneys," Harry reminded her.

"Then I'd rather walk the ten miles than spend another moment with you," she said flatly.

He deserved that. Not only had he failed to wed an heiress and save his family from financial ruin, Harry had also hurt one of his sister's best friends in the most roguish way possible.

"I'll see if Mr. Somers will take you home."

The solicitor, who had watched the dramatic proceedings unfold with obvious discomfort, stood a safe distance from Harry and Tina whilst awaiting his carriage from the nearby mews.

Tina shot Harry a suspicious look. "Aren't you going to summon a hackney for yourself?"

He shook his head. "I didn't get to finish my proposal."

"Don't you need to find Lady Regina for that?" His sister scoffed. "Bianca's not an heiress anymore, remember?"

"Bianca's money isn't why I want to marry her," he said quietly.

Tina tilted her head. "You're really going to ask for her hand despite everything?"

"Do you wish I would not?"

"I adore Bianca," Tina answered hotly.

"As do I. However, there are practical concerns

that directly affect you. Such as, failing to secure a large dowry means we shan't be able to afford any more seasons in London. We won't be able to afford much of anything, as a matter of fact. The items currently in your armoire will have to last forever. And you'll have to marry for love as well, because there's no blunt to give you a dowry, or even a—"

"You wish to marry for love?" his sister repeated, her voice soft. "If that is the case, I will happily patch every moth hole in my increasingly unfashionable wardrobe until I, too, am lucky enough to marry a man *I* choose, rather than one who chooses my dowry."

"She hasn't accepted me yet," he pointed out wryly. "Or even allowed me to ask the question."

Tina made a pained face. "I don't think today's your day. Bianca needs an opportunity to come to grips with her current situation before she can be expected to—"

A loud scream rent the air.

"Help!" shouted a panicked female voice from the other side of the Gladwells' closed front door. "Help! Come quick!"

Harry, Tina, and Mr. Somers all raced back up the walkway. Harry was the first to the front step. He turned the handle and wrenched open the door.

Bianca lay just inside the threshold, her limbs crumpled and lifeless.

A half-eaten apple rolled from her limp fingers and bounced against the toe of Harry's boot. He dropped to his knees at once, moving white-faced

Goose aside so that he could place his cheek near Bianca's nose and mouth, to feel for breath. He pressed his ear to her bosom in hopes of hearing her heart beat.

"What happened?" he asked hoarsely.

"I don't know!" Goose babbled in obvious panic. "I came back from delivering the apples to the kitchen, and found Bianca just like this!"

"Apples? What are you talking about?"

"The sack of apples Lady Quinseley brought. She found them in our front garden—"

"Goose, you don't have apple trees!"

Harry snatched up the half-eaten apple and gave it a careful sniff. Something was off. He peered carefully at the fruit's scab-colored exterior. His eyes widened to discover several puncture marks in its juicy flesh.

"It's poisoned," he growled. "Tina, go with Goose to the kitchen and throw out all the apples. Mr. Somers, I see your carriage has arrived. Go at once to the closest surgeon and bring him back here posthaste."

"And you?" Tina asked softly.

"I'm not leaving Bianca's side." Harry stared at them all. "What are you waiting for? Go!"

The others scattered at once.

Harry scooped Bianca up into his arms and cradled her to his chest. There on the entranceway floor, he rocked her close, murmuring words of encouragement and love and growing desperation as he kept an ear cocked toward the open door in hopes of hearing Mr. Somers return with a doctor in tow.

Tina arrived first, with Goose at her side.

"None of the other apples have puncture marks or smell funny," Tina murmured to Harry. "We threw them out anyway."

He grunted. "Good."

To the devil with Lady Quinseley! Whether Bianca pulled through or not, Harry intended to march the wicked countess before the magistrate and—

Oh, God, what if Bianca didn't pull through?

Carriage wheels sounded outside. Harry snapped his head toward the open door. It was not Mr. Somers' coach, but a hackney. A distinguished older man with a surgeon's leather tool case exited the carriage.

"What happened to Mr. Somers?" Tina asked in confusion.

"Who cares?" Harry growled. "Help is finally here."

"I'm Dr. Mayhew," said the surgeon when he reached the threshold. "May I see the patient?"

"You can do more than see her," Harry said stiffly. "I expect you to save her."

"I shall do my best." Dr. Mayhew set his tool case down beside Harry and knelt to the floor. "I don't mean to be indelicate about such matters, but are you able to pay for my services? Colleagues have warned me that your father—"

Harry shoved his hand into his pocket, pulled

out his mother's ring, and slapped it into the doctor's open hand. "Solid gold should do."

Tina gasped. "But that was to be Bianca's wedding ring!"

"Not if she never wakes up," Harry said grimly.

The doctor closed his fingers around the ring, sighed, then handed it back. "Give me the girl and a bit of space, if you don't mind."

Harry made the transfer and scrambled back out of Dr. Mayhew's way. "If she dies, you die."

Tina grabbed his arm. "You cannot threaten doctors who—"

"It is no idle threat. It is a solemn vow."

To his credit, Dr. Mayhew did not allow the threat of impending homicide to distract him from examining his patient and the apple that she had consumed.

"It's laudanum," he said grimly. "The apple appears to have been soaked in it."

"Laudanum," Harry repeated. Soldiers and civilians alike took droplets of the stuff to curb pain and banish insomnia.

"It's not usually fatal in low doses," the surgeon explained to Tina. "But since we don't know how much Miss White has consumed… "

"What can be done to counteract its ill effects?" Harry demanded.

"Nothing," Dr. Mayhew replied. "All we can do now is wait and see."

CHAPTER 26

*B*ianca was floating face-down in the still waters of a vast sea, gazing sightlessly into the endless dark depths stretching before her.

There was something she was supposed to do, something she needed to remember, but all she could think about was the devastating news that there was no dowry after all. No reason for Harry to still want to marry her.

She would be a maidservant for the rest of her life. Perhaps to the Gladwells, if she was lucky. To someone like Lady Quinseley, if she were not. Lady Quinseley... Was that what she was supposed to remember?

"... if you would only just... " A muffled pause. "... *please...* "

It was not the countess's voice carried along the black currents surrounding Bianca. It was Harry's voice, soft and urgent and pleading and frightened. How silly! Nothing frightened Harry. He was a devil-may-care rakehell. The very definition of flip-pant and carefree.

"… Bianca, I am begging… So sorry for all that I've done… " An even longer pause. "… cannot bear to be without you… "

Bears! That's what it was. A mama bear, a papa bear, and a baby bear—no, that wasn't it; that made no sense at all. *Seven* bears, not three. No, it was seven doors. No, seven *apples*. But where would the apples have come from? There were no apple trees at the Gladwells' cottage. Perhaps the sack had been full of pears or plums or gooseberries. Her lips still tasted like…

Tears. Her lips tasted like tears. Damp and salty and warm with a familiar pressure. It was a kiss. She was being kissed! These were Harry's lips upon hers, firm where she was soft, strong where she was weak, pulling her up out of the water and away from the tide until—

A loud, sucking gasp exploded from Bianca's throat and her eyes flew open.

Harry's startled gaze was inches from hers, his eyes at first shocked, then glassy, then smiling in disbelief.

"What… " she managed, the word barely audible.

"Thank God." Harry crushed her to his chest, wrapping his strong arms tight around her. "I thought I'd lost you."

She touched her thumb to her fingertips. The pads of her fingers were sticky. The apple! She'd been eating an apple when… when…

"What happened?" She lifted her head from Harry's chest to look at him.

His expression darkened. "Lady Quinseley poisoned you."

Bianca gasped. "Poisoned me!"

"As soon as I can bear to leave your side, my first stop will be to the magistrate." Harry's hands gripped her shoulders, his blue gaze intense. "Are you all right?"

Bianca realized she was reclining on his lap in the middle of her bed in the Gladwells' guest chamber... and that an unknown man was watching them.

She pushed away from Harry and scrambled to her feet.

"That may have looked like a compromising position, but I was just... he was just... " she stammered..

The man stepped forward. "I'm here to help you, not judge you. I'm Doctor Mayhew. You gave us quite a scare."

Bianca held still as the doctor pressed the backs of his fingers to her forehead to check for fever, then lifted her wrist to count her pulse.

As soon as Doctor Mayhew pronounced her healthy and took his leave from them, Harry closed the guest chamber door and locked it, then turned to Bianca.

"I wouldn't care if we *had* been compromised," he said fiercely.

"Of course you would," she chided him. "You—"

"Bianca, nothing in this world matters to me as much as you do. A life without you is a world without sunlight. It cannot be borne." He grasped her hands. "Marry me."

"You cannot mean it."

"*Marry me.*" He kissed the backs of her fingers, then clasped her hands to his chest. "I implore you."

"I have no fortune," she reminded him.

"You are *my* good fortune," he corrected her softly. "My happiest moments have been with you. By your side, I am able to be my true self. Not a title, not a fortune-hunter, but a man desperately, irrevocably, wholeheartedly in love with you."

Her pulse fluttered. "I would be your ruin."

"You would be my salvation."

"We would be shunned by many of your peers. All of the reasons my father did not marry my mother despite his wealth and their love still hold true for you and me. You are an earl, Harry. Heir to a marquessate. I am no one."

"You are wrong. You are everything."

"Without a dowry, I am nothing more than my mother's daughter. Lady Regina accused me of prowling the beau monde in search of a protector. She meant to be cruel, but that does not make her wrong. A woman in my position—"

"You're not listening to me."

"You're not making any sense! You've spent a lifetime hunting the largest dowry in the ton. And if your search has led you to Lady Regina... Why would you settle for an illegitimate orphan without so much as a farthing?"

"Why would I settle for a life of misery with a lady I cannot stand, instead of a lifetime of love with the woman whose face brings me joy every time I glimpse it? You cannot offer me a dowry. Fair enough. Nor can I offer you luxury and wealth. If you marry me, our lives will be rich with love, not gold. For me, it is more than enough. The only question is whether *I* am a sufficient catch for *you*."

"Any woman would be lucky to have you, but you cannot say the same about me. Lady Regina would not take well to being thrown over for one such as me. She will respond as cruelly as she is able, and incite anyone who will listen to do the same."

"I do not give a fat fig about being in Lady Regina's good graces. Anyone who no longer wishes to associate with me because I chose my heart over my purse, to them I say good riddance. The only good opinion I care for is yours." He pressed a kiss to each of her palms. "I love you, Bianca. Now and always. If you do not feel the same—"

"Of course I feel the same," she burst out. "How do you think the thought of you marrying Lady Regina—"

"There is only one woman I want to be my wife. *You*, Bianca. You, and only you. No one else will do. I know exactly what it will mean to marry you. It will mean that I get to spend the rest of my life with the woman I love. Could there be any greater fortune than that? At long last, I've found what I have been searching for." He touched his thumb to her cheek. "She's standing right before me."

Bianca's lungs tightened with desperate hope. Could it be true? After a lifetime spent hunting the biggest dowry, could Harry truly choose her—choose *love*—over the promise of wealth?

Harry fumbled in his pocket and pulled out a slender gold ring.

"I have been waiting for the right moment… and the right woman," he said gruffly. "I love you, Bianca. You are my world and you have my heart. I cannot offer you a life of ease and riches, but I can promise you that my heart beats solely for you. Every breath I take for the rest of my life, belongs to you. You will make me the most fortunate of huntsmen if you agree to be my wife." His eyes sought hers as he held up the ring. "What do you say?"

"Yes," she said breathlessly, the word coming out little more than a gasp. "*Yes*."

He slid the ring onto her finger then pressed his lips to hers.

"Oh, how I love you," he murmured against her mouth.

"I love *you*," she whispered back, and kissed him.

She wrapped her arms around Harry's neck, reveling in his warmth, his strength, his solidness. He was choosing her, was offering himself. He was hers, just as her heart was his.

It did not matter what Lady Regina and Lady

Quinseley and the rest of Polite Society wanted. Bianca and Harry had what they wanted: each other. They had love, which made them richer than most of their peers. They had the rest of their lives to fill with kisses just like this one.

Happily ever after.

EPILOGUE

The guest chamber door flew open. All seven of Bianca's friends tumbled inside. She leapt out of Harry's embrace, her heart pounding wildly.

"Knock next time," she gasped. "We could have been…"

"Kissing," finished Harry, with an anything-but-subtle wink.

Goose clapped her hands. "You were dead, but now you're not!"

All of the girls crowded around Bianca, hugging her in obvious relief.

"We had to see for ourselves," Joy explained.

"And we have news that couldn't wait." Peavy leaned out through the open doorway and motioned for someone further down the corridor to join them.

"What couldn't wait?" Bianca asked in confusion.

Harry laced his fingers with hers. "Bianca and I have news, too."

"You'll want to hear this first." Peavy pulled an older gentleman into the crowded guest chamber. "Tell them, Father."

It was Mr. Somers, who had been playing cards with Mr. Gladwell when Lady Quinseley arrived with her sack of apples to inform Bianca she was no longer an heiress… and to ruin her life.

Mr. Somers thanked his daughter, and pulled a rolled column of yellowed parchment out from beneath his lapel. He cleared his throat, then turned to Bianca. "I found my original copy of the terms to Miss White's dowry."

"Which expired on my twenty-first birthday," Bianca said bitterly.

"Not quite." Mr. Somers unrolled the parchment and pointed at a line, three paragraphs down. "The dowry revokes *after* you're twenty-one."

Bianca frowned. "Isn't that what I said?"

"Partially." He read the passage aloud, slowly, his eyes shining. "You just had your twenty-first birthday, but you won't turn twenty-two for another full year."

She stared at him, her hand suddenly clammy in Harry's. "You're saying… "

Mr. Somers beamed at her. "Congratulations, Miss White. You're still an heiress."

Bianca let out a whoop and threw her arms about Harry in victory.

He swirled her in a wide circle and pressed his lips to hers, kissing her with renewed passion.

"Oh dear," said Doc, her voice loud and teasing. "This certainly seems like a compromising situation. I'm afraid with this many witnesses, you two shall be forced to marry."

Without taking her lips from Harry's, Bianca flung out the hand with the engagement ring.

"They're already betrothed!" Tina squealed in rapture.

Joy, Goose, Doc, and Peavy cheered.

Rosie sneezed.

Miss Drowsy murmured something unintelligible, climbed onto the guest room bed, and fell asleep.

Bianca and Harry laughed, and kissed again, then danced the others around the room, banging into furniture and laughing in delight.

When the celebrations slowed, Mr. Somers handed Bianca the contract. "Do forgive my tardiness. I would have brought this to you faster, but my first stop was to Bow Street."

Her breath caught. "Will the Runners take action against Lady Quinseley?"

"They already have. Bow Street Runners collected the countess from her home and have placed her in a holding cell to await trial." His smile was fatherly. "She won't be bothering you again, Miss White."

"But you'll bother *her* plenty," added Goose, her twinkling eyes mischievous. "Once you become a marchioness, you won't just have won—you'll outrank her!"

"Lady Quinseley will hate that more than the prison cell," Doc agreed with a chuckle. "It'll eat her alive."

"I'll never have to worry about her again," Bianca repeated in disbelief and joy.

"We have a much better future to look forward to." Harry placed her fingers around his upper arm and raised his brows. "Shall we take a turn about Hyde Park and show off the new jewelry on your finger?"

"We'll come with you," Goose shouted. "We're all invited to the wedding, right?"

"Of course," Bianca said with a laugh. "As long as you promise to invite me to each of yours."

Tina smiled at her bashfully. "It could happen sooner than you think."

FOR EVEN MORE FUN-FILLED ROMANCE, featuring a found family of caper-committing siblings, don't miss the rollicking **Wild Wynchesters**!

Why seduce a duke the normal way, when you can accidentally kidnap one in an elaborately planned heist?

Do it all in The Duke Heist!

LOVE Romance? Grab a FREE book!

Sign up at http://ridley.vip for members-only exclusives!

Missing an Erica Ridley book?
Grab the latest edition of the free, downloadable and printable complete book list by series here:
https://ridley.vip/booklist

THANK YOU

AND SNEAK PEEKS

THANK YOU FOR READING

Love talking books with fellow readers?

Join the *Historical Romance Book Club* for prizes, books, and live chats with your favorite romance authors:

Facebook.com/groups/HistRomBookClub

Check out the **Patreon** for bonus content, sneak peeks, advance review copies and more:

https://www.patreon.com/EricaRidleyFans

And don't miss the **official website**:

www.EricaRidley.com/books

ABOUT THE AUTHOR

Erica Ridley is a *New York Times* and *USA Today* best-selling author of witty, feel-good historical romance novels, including THE DUKE HEIST, featuring the Wild Wynchesters. Why seduce a duke the normal way, when you can accidentally kidnap one in an elaborately planned heist?

In the *12 Dukes of Christmas* series, enjoy witty, heartwarming Regency romps nestled in a picturesque snow-covered village. After all, nothing heats up a winter night quite like finding oneself in the arms of a duke!

Two popular series, the *Dukes of War* and *Rogues to Riches*, feature roguish peers and dashing war heroes who find love amongst the splendor and madness of Regency England.

When not reading or writing romances, Erica can be found eating couscous in Morocco, ziplining through rainforests in Central America, or getting hopelessly lost in the middle of Budapest.

～

Let's be friends! Find Erica on:
www.EricaRidley.com